David Tetlow was born in Rossendale, Lancashire, during the Second World War. Following his school years, he worked in mechanical engineering and later specialised in textile machinery research and development.

He is married to Joyce and has a son, a daughter and four grandchildren. He joined the Lancashire police during the 1960s and completed most of his thirty years' service in Greater Manchester, where he retired as an Investigating Officer.

To GRAHAM AND PAULINE.

BEST WISHES

DAVE

Dedication

To Joyce

David Tetlow

BEWARE MY SHADOW

AUSTIN MACAULEY PUBLISHERS™

LONDON • CAMBRIDGE • NEW YORK • SHARJAH

A CIP catalogue record for this title is available from the British Library.

ISBN 9781788235884 (Paperback)
ISBN 9781788235891 (Hardback)
ISBN 9781788235907 (E-Book)

www.austinmacauley.com

First Published (2018)
Austin Macauley Publishers Ltd™
25 Canada Square
Canary Wharf
London
E14 5LQ

Acknowledgements

Thanks to Kay, Sarah and David for their support, and Lee and Paul for their help.

Chapter One

It was four o'clock in the morning, on the first Sunday of May, in the year of the Millennium, it had been a quiet night around Josh Delany's house, a semi-detached in the small Lancastrian town of Clayton, a few miles from the county's palatine city of Lancaster where he worked as a policeman. He had slept heavily, probably due to tiredness and slight intoxication, until a loud banging noise jerked him awake.

'What the hell?' he shouted as he got out of bed and glowered through the bedroom window overlooking his front door and saw a filthy dishevelled-looking object staring up at his bedroom window, 'What the hell are you doing here, Baldy?' he shouted at the spectacle.

'Wife's chucked me out again,' it shouted back, 'I need somewhere to kip.'

He let Baldy in through the kitchen door. 'Look at the state of you, you look like you've been dragged through a hedge backwards,' he said, and, indeed, Baldy was in a sorry state, as hairless on top as his nickname suggested, with several days' growth of beard and filthy, crumpled clothing. He smelled strongly of sweat, alcohol and other indescribable odours.

'I'm absolutely knackered,' Baldy said.

'When did she throw you out and why, may I ask?'

'It's a long story but nowt new,' he said. 'I got bladdered last night, and she threw me out, I've been sleeping in your shed.'

'In my shed?'

'Yea, but it's been cold, and I need a proper kip; anyway; you should lock that shed of yours, all sorts of undesirables can get in there.'

'None as undesirable as you I bet.'

Delany packed him off to his bed, with strict instructions to shower before he got in and to throw his filthy clothing through the back bedroom window. He was slightly bigger than Baldy, but Baldy would have to make do with some of his old clothes when he awoke.

He made sure that Baldy was aware that his daughters were visiting the next evening and that he wanted him long gone before then.

As Baldy went upstairs, Delany decided that he may as well stay up now as he was on duty at 7am. He sat having breakfast and began to reflect on their strange relationship, he had known Baldy for most of his fifteen years' police service. Baldy had, for most of his life, been a career criminal, having convictions for assault, theft and burglary stretching back to his teenage years.

He was now in his early sixties. Delany had arrested him on two occasions for burglary, and on each occasion, he had admitted twenty or thirty other offences; he had spent at least ten of his sixty-odd years in prison.

On being released from his latest spell some eight years before, he had approached Delany in a public house and said that he was getting too old for prison and intended to go straight. Their relationship developed, with Delany meeting him in the pub and pumping him for information about other local criminals.

Baldy giving whatever information he wanted to give, mainly about thugs who had offended him in some way, and being paid for that information in drinks.

However, as time went on, Delany had seen another side of Baldy, a quirkiness and even a degree of humour which appealed to him. During the past few years, they had become friends, with Delany looking out for Baldy and trying, where possible, to keep him on as straight and narrow a path as was possible given his nature and propensity to drink excessively.

At 6am that bright summer Sunday morning, Inspector Delany was driving to work, Lancaster Central Police Station, for his final tour of duty in the police.

It was the first year of the new Millennium, and he was retiring from the police after fifteen years; on the face of it, not a long time, but he had spent twenty years before that in the army, which had counted towards his pension, and he had felt for some time that it was time for him to do something other than work in such disciplined environments; after all, he was now fifty-three years old.

He had thought seriously of staying until he was sixty, the maximum for his rank, until he was offered a job with a local firm of solicitors. When the offer came, at first, he had turned it down, thinking that they wanted to use his experience against his former colleagues and friends, but they assured him that the job would be the investigation of possible fraudulent civil claims against their insurance branch, and that had swayed his decision.

On arrival, he found, as he had expected, that the main job of the morning was supervising the demolition of a factory chimney at an old redundant cotton mill just around the corner from the station.

This was a rare event in the city, and a considerable crowd was expected; the safety of these people was his priority, and, as such, he had previously ordered barriers to be delivered to the site. After instructing his sergeant and constables in their duties, they made their way to the factory yard.

They arrived at the yard at 7.30am, where he spoke to the demolition expert, a man known locally as Blaster Jones. Jones was a large, imposing man of middle age, and he obviously knew his business.

Delany asked Jones where he should place the barriers to control the crowd. They stood close, and looking up at the great monolith, Jones said in his broad Lancashire accent,

'As you can imagine, lad, it's been stood there for well over a hundred years, and for most of that time, this was a working factory. A hundred years' worth of smoke has come out of that thing; we will detonate at exactly ten o'clock. Look,' he said, 'Walk along here with me.'

They strode off across the factory yard and away from the chimney, and at about one hundred yards, Jones stopped and said,

'The last few bricks will fall just about here,' he bent and put a chalk-cross on the ground.

'So,' Delany said, 'we will put the barriers about fifty yards that way,' pointing away from the spot.

'Oh no,' Jones said, with a knowing smile, tut-tutting and shaking his head in the way that experts do, 'Walk with me again, lad.'

They walked another sixty yards across the yard, where Jones again stopped, spat on his fingers to test the wind direction and put a second chalk-mark on the ground.

'As I said, that thing has been pumping out smoke for a hundred years, not only that, birds, rats, mice, spiders and other vermin have been living in and around that thing all that time. As it crashes to the ground, a great cloud of soot, bird muck, spider webs and other various filth will rise up about fifty feet into the air and settle here, your barriers should be about fifty yards that way.'

Delany thanked Jones and instructed his team where to erect the barriers.

Time went on, and the crowd gathered, more, in fact, than Delany had anticipated; not that it was a problem, there was plenty of room at the back of the great yard for everyone.

At 9.30am, Delany estimated that there were about 500 people behind his barriers and that all was going well.

With just fifteen minutes to go, Delany saw, to his astonishment, two police figures walking towards them from the direction of the chimney; they were the local Superintendent and Chief Inspector.

His surprise was mainly due to the fact that uniformed officers of those ranks did not normally work on the weekend. In fact, to see them outside of nine to five, Monday to Friday, unless there was some kind of an emergency, was a rare event indeed.

He decided that courtesy demanded that he go meet them, and as he walked towards them, he admitted to himself that they looked splendid. Their uniforms, rarely worn outside the police station where they were normally kept on coat hangers, were pristine, both were carrying swagger sticks, and at that moment, the sun came out, glinting on their shiny buttons, cap braids and epaulettes.

Delany also reflected on the two men and their differences. The Superintendent William Baxter, who was vastly overweight and walked with a slight waddle, was greatly disliked by Delany and, indeed, by most of the people he was in charge of.

He was known by the officers as effing Billy, not because he was fraternal, friendly and full of fun, but because of his propensity to swear a lot. He also suffered from the nine o'clock shudders, often to be heard saying, 'They shudder done this, or they shudder done that,' after enjoying his quiet weekend at home.

Some also called him puffing Billy because of his weight and general lack of fitness. He had made life very uncomfortable for Delany during the two years they had worked together. Delany had thought of protesting until he had realised that effing Billy made life uncomfortable for everybody.

Chief Inspector Colin Bingley was a gentleman well respected by the staff, very fit and a regular running partner of Delany, whom he had grown quite fond of.

He approached the two men, pointed out the first chalk-mark and explained that was where the last brick was expected to fall, at which Baxter shouted, 'Mr Delany, the crowd you have there are quite unruly. Look, kids are climbing on the barriers, running 'round them and people are spilling out at the side, this is quite unacceptable; get back there, and sort them out now!'

Delany saw that the two men were standing about halfway between the two chalk-marks. He began to say, 'But, sir, let me tell you.'

Baxter broke in and shouted, 'No ifs, no buts, Mister Delany. Get back there, and do as I tell you now.'

Delany looked at a point above Baxter's head and shouted, 'Yes, sir.' A habit from his army days whenever an order was given by an incompetent that he disagreed with.

Delany walked back to the barriers, where he and his colleagues soon sorted out the crowd, and time moved on. At five minutes to ten, the two men were still standing at the halfway point between the two chalk-marks, and Jimmy Wilcox, the sergeant, spoke to Delany.

'Don't you think that we had better warn them about the predicament they are in, sir?'

'I tried Jimmy, but Billy would not listen.'

As ten o'clock approached, Delany's emotions were torn with the angel sitting on his right shoulder, saying, 'Go and warn Mr Bingley, he's a mate of yours, you think the world of him.'

But the devil was sitting on his left shoulder, saying, 'This is the moment you have been waiting for during the last two years; enjoy it, you'll never get another chance like this. Baxter's been a pain in the backside ever since you first saw him, let him stew.'

The devil won the argument.

At ten o'clock exactly, there was an enormous bang, and the chimney slowly toppled towards them, the last brick landed a few feet behind the first chalk-mark and rolled almost on top of it. Jones had been precise.

Then, as predicted, a great cloud of filth rose fifty feet into the air, and the prevailing breeze blew it gently, but surely, towards the two men between the chalk-marks. They immediately saw their dilemma, and Delany heard Bingley shout, 'Run for it.' Then he heard Baxter shout, 'Walk, man, where's your dignity?' But Bingley had already taken off like a hare.

Baxter began to walk, or at least waddle, quickly away from the threatening cloud, but unfortunately for him, not quickly enough. The cloud engulfed him and he disappeared completely from view as it descended to the ground.

Bingley easily beat the cloud to the second chalk-mark, but when Baxter emerged a few seconds later, he no longer resembled the smartly dressed officer of before. He was now covered from cap to boots in black filth. The crowd, who had attended to watch a great spectacle, were now treated to an additional marvellous slapstick comedy. Those with cameras were snapping away, and the crowd was completely in hysterics with laughter.

The two officers did not stay to enjoy the theatre they had been a part of but strode off quickly towards the police station.

On his return to the police station, Delany expected all kinds of trouble from Baxter, but, instead, and to his relief, he found that both officers had left for home; Baxter, no doubt, to have a bath and clean up.

Chapter Two

That evening was Delany's farewell party and a crowd had gathered in the force headquarters police club. He was delighted with the number and the age group of his workmates who had turned out, a mixture of uniform and detective officers.

He had never got used to the fact that his popularity with the constables and sergeants he had commanded stemmed from the fact that he was willing, as their boss, to face as much responsibility and danger as themselves. They were aware that their next boss would most likely regard himself/herself as a desk-bound manager.

Chief Inspector Bingley had offered his services as the speaker, and as he entered the club, he approached Delany and said, 'Baxter was not very happy this morning. I don't think we will see him tonight, did you know what was about to happen?'

'Yes, well, I had an idea. I did try to tell Baxter, but you were there, and he, as usual, would not listen. Sorry, I should have made more of an effort to warn you, but I knew you would be quick enough to get away.'

'To be honest with you, Josh, I quite enjoyed it. He had that coming for a long time, and I'm glad you let him have it.'

Bingley was later to speak on Delany's behalf; however, that would not come until the guests were all well-oiled and receptive. Delany circulated among the 100 or so people in the room, becoming more and more surprised at his popularity which may or may not have been from the fact that he enjoyed and bought at least one drink for those at each table.

At about 10pm, Bingley got to his feet, and the room went silent. He started with a bit of history, commenting on the fact that Josh had joined the Royal Marines at the age of eighteen. 'It was rumoured', he said, 'that Josh had spent the majority of his army service in the Special Air Service, but Josh has never confirmed this, even to me, and I regard him as a friend as well as a colleague, so maybe it was just a rumour.'

'But', he said, 'because of Josh's ability in the early years of his police service to work under cover and to infiltrate local and national criminal gangs, I do not think so.'

However, he felt sure, knowing Josh, that he would not wish him to dwell on this. Josh, he said, had spent five years in each rank, constable sergeant and inspector. Time, of course, had been against him, having joined the police at the age of thirty-eight. Had he joined at eighteen or nineteen, who knows what rank he would have attained.

He continued to praise and joke about Josh's time in the police. He finished by saying, 'Josh is a good friend. But as I'm sure you are all aware by now of what happened this morning, beware anyone who makes an enemy out of him.'

This comment caused a huge laugh and cheer.

Delany reflected on all this in the taxi on his way home. He wished his wife, Helen, could have been there, she had been killed in a hit-and-run car crash some four years before, and he missed her terribly.

Every night when he went to bed, he thought of her, and the pain, even after four years, had not gone away. He let himself into his house. Thinking of her now, even though he had enjoyed his evening, he felt as he always did when he walked in the house: lonely and dispirited.

Suddenly, he remembered that his daughters, Holly and Beverley, were coming home the next afternoon; Holly from her university in Manchester, where she was studying law; and Beverley, who was slightly older, was also coming from Manchester, where she was a constable in the local police.

Holly was bringing home her boyfriend Harry, who was also at Manchester University, to meet her father for the first time; this thought cheered him up immensely. Holly and Beverley were the people in his life; since the death of his wife, they mattered to him more than anything else in the world.

He decided to have a little whisky before bed and searched for the full bottle he knew was in the cupboard. It was empty, 'Bloody Baldy,' he shouted. He went upstairs to find Baldy fast asleep in his bed.

He went to the bed in the spare room, and before he dropped off to sleep, his last thought was, *Harry had better be worthy of my Holly or there will be hell to pay.*

Chapter Three

The following morning, as he relaxed in his favourite chair, with Baldy still asleep upstairs, that period of his life came vividly back to his mind when he had first got the news that Helen had been killed in a fail-to-stop road crash. Some people called them accidents, but the word accident brought to mind something that was unavoidable. This crash and death was completely avoidable if the slightest of care and attention had been taken by the other driver.

Helen had been a lecturer in English at the University of Manchester and had been to a late evening conference at the university. She had telephoned him at eleven in the evening to say the conference was over and that, as it was a Friday and as they both had the weekend off, rather than staying over at the university, she would travel home so they could enjoy a full weekend together.

He had decided to wait up for her. As it happened, he fell asleep on the sofa. At two o'clock that morning, he was awakened by a knocking on the door, and as soon as he saw it was Colin Bingley, who, at that time, was the local traffic inspector, he knew something was seriously wrong. The inspector gave him the awful news that his wife had been in a car crash along the top road approaching the town near to Nibs Quarry.

Her car had apparently been pushed off the road by another vehicle and had hit a tree head on; she had died at the scene and had been transferred to the mortuary following the crash.

The next few days, he could hardly recall because of the numbness and desolation that had descended upon him, coming to terms with the fact that he would not see his beloved Helen in this life again. He also had to face telling his teenage daughters that their mother was gone from their lives. They were both equally devastated.

It was only after the formalities of the funeral were over that he could start to think about what had happened during the crash and the subsequent investigation.

He arranged an interview with Bingley, thanked him for breaking the news in person about his wife's death and asked how the investigation was going.

Bingley informed him that Helen had been driving home, and as she drove along near the top of Nibs Quarry, it appeared that she was overtaken by a Vauxhall Nova, they knew it was a blue Nova because paint samples transferred to Helen's car. The Nova had collided with the offside of her car, near a sharp left-hand bend, throwing her car off to the left, through the wooden fence and over the quarry side where it had hit a tree and stopped. He said, 'Had it not hit the tree, it would have plunged into the water of the flooded quarry.'

Delany said, 'How did you find it at that time of the day?'

'Someone passing noticed the fence debris on the road and rang in,' Bingley replied.

From the tyre marks on the road, it seemed, explained Bingley, that the Nova had gone into a long skid, suggesting that it had been travelling very fast. It had also collided with the fence lower down the road and had been fortunate not to go over the side and into the quarry.

The driver had then driven away from the scene without reporting the crash or making any attempt to assist the other driver. They were, he said, making enquiries to trace the Nova with all the local garages as it must have been extensively damaged. Bingley concluded by saying that they'd had no luck yet and that he would appreciate any help he could get.

Sometime later over a few pints in the Horse and Farrier, he discussed the whole thing with Baldy who promised to help.

One week later, Baldy came to his house, where he told Delany that on that particular Friday night, a gang of the local motor heads had been holding a "race meeting", where they met together just before midnight, after spending the evening in the local pubs, and held an illegal point-to-point time trial in the local countryside.

The course he had found out was about twenty miles long, and it included the spot where Helen had died. More than that, he related, one of the idiots, a lad they called Jazz Anders, had owned a blue Nova, which he had apparently sold.

Further to that, Baldy said that he had seen Anders and said, 'He looks like he's got broken ribs or summat and his legs in plaster.' Baldy added that Jazz's car had a personal number plate JAZ 14.

Delany took this information to Bingley, who, in turn, promised to investigate. Delany's leaving remark was 'please keep me informed'. Bingley promised he would do so.

Two weeks later, Bingley visited Delany in his office and told him that they had identified Jazz Anders' real name, James Michael Anders, a local disqualified driver with dozens of traffic convictions.

He had admitted that when he was disqualified some weeks before, he had owned a blue Nova which, he says, he sold to a man in a pub. 'The usual crap they come out with,' said Bingley, 'He says he does not know who the man was, he simply paid cash and drove it away.'

Anders had the injuries which had caused the suspicion, but further checks had revealed that during that particular period of time, he had been in a hospital bed in the local infirmary and could not possibly be involved in that crash.

His injuries were from a previous crash, which had not been reported to the police and which he refused to expand upon. Anders had been reported for several traffic offences but could not have been the driver at the time of his wife's death.

'What about his personal number plate? There's no way he would have sold that with the car,' said Delany.

'Yes, we thought about that, but he insists that he did,' replied Bingley.

'Did you know about the race meetings?'

'I know where you're going with there. They constantly change the venues, sometimes the pubs they meet in and the roads they race on. It's been on my mind ever since Helen died. Could we have prevented it from happening? I wish I knew the answer. We did get some information; we now know that they mainly meet in the Butchers Arms at Barton booth, generally on Friday evenings.'

On his drive home that evening, Delany thought about what had been said and decided that criticism of the Traffic Department would solve no problems. He also thought that although Anders was clearly not the driver, his car had been involved and Anders knew who was. 'What next?' he said out loud to himself.

Chapter Four

Two weeks after the crash at eight o'clock on Friday evening, a bent old man in shabby clothing, with grey hair, a pale unshaven face and several days' growth of beard, with the aid of two elbow crutches, limped into the Butchers Arms at Barton booth, sat gratefully by the side of the fire in the tap room and ordered a pint of the local beer.

'Quiet tonight,' he said to the barman.

'Yea, they'll all be in later,' he replied.

The old man sat quietly, sipping his beer. About nine o'clock, a group of rowdy young men entered. They had obviously been drinking elsewhere. One of the young men was limping badly and using a walking stick. They got their drinks and sat close to the old man, without even noticing him.

As the evening went on, the pub filled, and the young man with the limp was obviously becoming more and more drunk and agitated. He suddenly shouted at another youth alongside him, 'You bastard. I covered for you after you nearly bloody killed me.'

The barman, fearing trouble, shouted, 'Calm down, Jazz, we don't want any bother.'

'Sorry, Jim, there won't be any bother,' said the youth.

He began to talk to the other youth, quietly. The old man leaned forward to pick up his drink, he looked towards some men playing darts, apparently, unconcerned with the altercation.

Jazz said, 'I could not care less about the bloody car, they're ten a penny, we buy 'em cheap and we wreck 'em, that's the name of the game. But my bloody number plate you could have taken off before you shoved it in the Nib.'

The old man turned, had a glance at the youth Jazz had spoken to, finished his pint, stood up and limped out of the pub. Outside, Delany saw that there was no one about, straightened up, tucked the crutches under his arm and walked quickly to his car, which was parked two streets away, and drove home.

The following morning, Delany entered the collator's office at the county headquarters and picked up the files of local persistent motoring offenders. He soon picked out the file he was interested in, the man he had seen the night before with Anders.

William Craig, known as Craggy, was also a disqualified driver. It seemed that a car that had not been registered to, but reputed to belong to, Craig had been found wrecked and abandoned in Cumbria.

The local police had interviewed Craig, who had denied all knowledge. The date was two weeks before his wife's death and around the time of Jazz's injuries.

He made enquiries at the local hospital; it seemed that Jazz had been dropped off there with serious injuries by other young men who had left the hospital without any identification. An ambulance had not been used. Delany told Bingley of the possible whereabouts of the offending car.

Two days later, Bingley rang to say that he had employed a local police diver to confirm that Jazz's car was at the bottom of the Nib, they had pulled it out and paint scrapings showed that it was the car involved in his wife's death. But due to water immersion, there was no other evidence to be got from it.

'We have interviewed all the local motor heads that we are aware of. Nobody's saying anything, the number plates had only been stuck on by some kind of adhesive and came off when we raised the car. They are still at the bottom of the Nib, so, unfortunately, we cannot do Jazz the favour of returning them to him,' said Bingley.

'Colin,' Delany said, 'if you get a lad called William Craig in for any reason in the next week or so, will you let me know? I'd like to have a word.'

Bingley said, 'Yes, he's one of the lads we spoke to about your wife's death, he's a nasty sod, we got nowhere with him.'

One week later, Bingley contacted Delany to say that Craig was in custody. He had been arrested by a local traffic policeman, having been found disqualified-driving. Josh made his way to the cells, where, alone in an interview room, he spoke to Craig.

With a deadpan expression and a threatening voice, he said, 'I am Inspector Josh Delany. I know that you killed my wife in a crash near Nibs Quarry!'

Craig looking suddenly very scared. 'I want a solicitor.'

'Why, this is not a formal interview, there's no tape recorder going. I am just stating a fact. I don't even want you to admit it to me. I'll call in Inspector Bingley, and you can tell him all about it.'

'No chance.'

'Listen, scumbag, if you want to get rid of my shadow, I strongly advise you tell Mr Bingley the truth, you were the driver when my wife was run off the road. Do you understand?'

Craig relaxed, 'You've no evidence, have you?' He became cocky, saying, 'I'm being done for dizzy-driving, a fine at the most. If I admit that I smashed into your missus with Jazz's car at Nibs, I'll be doing ten for death by dangerous. Why should I do that? No chance. I could not care less about your bitch. If you can prove it, prove it; otherwise, piss off.'

Delany seethed. He wanted to make this lout admit his crime, he wanted to beat the truth out of him, but he knew that violence, at that time, was not an option, and he quietly became cold and controlled and said, 'I'm giving you the chance to pay for your crime through the law. They might sentence you to seven or eight years, but you know, as well as I, that you'll be out in less than half that. Take it.'

At this point, Craig, knowing that there was no evidence against him, had recovered from his fear and felt firmly in charge of the interview and shouted, 'I do not give a stuff for you, for your wife, for the law or for anything else; whatever I've done, it's out of your reach. You can't prove it, or you would not be talking to me like this, go stuff yourself, tell Bingley to stuff himself and do not bother me again.'

Josh left the interview room, knowing that he had done all he could to make Craig pay for his actions lawfully. He was also certain that Craig was guilty as sin.

Delany thanked Bingley and said, 'Does anyone outside police and motor head circles know that it was Jazz's car that was involved?'

'No, not that I am aware of, it was not in the newspapers or anything like that.'

'Has anyone mentioned Jazz's car or Nibs Quarry to him whilst he's been here?'

'No, he's only been interviewed for dizzy-driving.'

That evening, Delany and Baldy had a drink together and discussed the interview. Baldy undertook to find out when the next point-to-point was being held and to formulate their next plan of action.

One week later on a bleak Friday in November, Baldy called on Delany to tell him that he had renewed his friendship with a man he had served time with whose son was one of the motor heads. 'He seems quite proud of it,' said Baldy.

'They are meeting next Friday at midnight, on a car park about a mile north of the Butchers Arms and doing a racing time trial over the lanes to the north of Lancaster taking in Nibs Quarry. It's about a twenty-mile run; apparently, the winner gets free booze from the others until the next meet.'

They discussed what was to be done.

During that week, Delany visited Nibs Quarry. He noted that there was a car park at the top of the quarry, offering a viewpoint across the nearby reservoirs, and as he followed the lane down from this, it became very steep along the quarry side for about half a mile until it came to a sharp, dog leg left-hand bend at the bottom of the quarry.

There were two warning signs: on the left of the roadside before the bend and another sign sprayed on the road surface. At the bend, there were chevrons across the bottom of the road before a wooden fence.

It was obvious that there had been several crashes there, as the chevrons and the fence were showing damage. Beyond the fence, there were bushes, rocks and, finally, the reservoir. Delany climbed the fence and broke several branches from the bushes and left them propped up behind the chevrons.

That Friday, he arrived at the quarry just as his watch was showing midnight, the conditions for his plan were perfect. A November night, very dark, no moon, no wind, cold, about five degrees, but not freezing. A few minutes later, he got a call from Baldy.

'They're at the car park, burning rubber; as they say, what a waste of good tyres, I'll ring when that first one sets off.'

Thirty minutes later, he rang again, 'First one's off, not our man.'

Delany waited, about eight minutes went by when he heard a car roaring in the distance; two minutes later, the lights of a Ford Escort came in sight at the top, on the quarry.

The driver screamed down the quarry side at an incredible speed, braking heavily as the driver spotted the signs for the bend and skidding around the bend, missing the chevrons by a couple of feet and roaring off into the night.

During the next twenty minutes, Delany witnessed two more cars perform in a similar manner.

Baldy rang and whispered into his phone, 'It's Craggy, he's off, no other car following.'

Delany knew that that meant there were no other cars than Craig's coming towards him. He ran to his own car, grabbed two black blankets under his arm and a large sack of leaves.

He ran up the lane, throwing the blankets over the first and second of the warning signs. He ran back down the lane, where he emptied the sack of leaves onto the road surface warning. He ran back to his car, where he took two large buckets full of ice cubes and threw them onto the road surface at the approach to the bend. He took the previously broken branches from the back of the chevrons and covered them. Delany then secreted himself in the bushes.

He had only been there a few seconds when he heard Craig's car coming his way. Craig screamed down the hill, as the others had done, clearly failed to see anything warning him of the bend until it was far too late. Delany later thought that he must have been doing about fifty miles per hour when he hit the ice and slammed sideways into the chevrons, smashing them asunder and slamming into the rocks beyond.

Delany quickly retrieved the blankets and buckets, brushed the remaining ice which was melting quickly; off the road, the speed of Craig's car had dispersed the leaves. He glanced at the wrecked car, saw that there was no movement, got into his own car and drove home.

The following morning, he got a call from Bingley to inform him of Craig's crash. 'Funny thing,' he said, 'I was working late and went to the scene about twenty minutes after it happened, and as I went through the broken fence, something crunched under my foot. I bent down and thought I felt some melting ice, even though it wasn't freezing. Strange, eh?'

Delany said, 'How's Craig?'

'Oh, he's alive, unlikely to walk again, his spinal cord was broken.'

Chapter Five

Delany woke with a start and realised that he had been dreaming. He went upstairs to find that Baldy had sprawled his filthy clothing across the bedroom floor. He was still in bed, asleep, but he did, however, appear to have showered.

Delany took the clothing and threw them through the bedroom window. He laid out clean clothing from his wardrobe, which were probably a size too big and went downstairs to incinerate the offending attire.

At 3pm that day, he woke Baldy and sent him packing. He had a shower and afterwards looked into the bedroom mirror and saw a man looking approximately right for his age. Five feet nine inches, salt and pepper hair, with a slim muscular frame, and he was overcritical with himself and said, 'You're looking flabby these days, lad, do something about it.'

Beverley arrived first. At twenty two years, she was the elder of the two; a pretty, dark-haired woman, tall at five feet seven inches, with a bubbling personality. She entered with a loud 'Hi, dad', a girl who could light up a room wherever she went. They spent the next hour discussing her love life, which she described as zero, and her career in the police, which was going well.

Holly arrived at about four thirty that day. She was twenty years old, very similar in looks to Beverley but with a completely different outlook on life; she was quieter and more introspective. Delany suspected that she was the cleverer of the two, but that he loved them equally, was apparent for anyone to see. She walked into the house, followed by a very sheepish-looking Harry, another twenty-year-old student. He looked as if he wished the earth would swallow him.

Holly said, 'Dad, this is Harry Woodstock, my significant other.'

They shook hands, and after a large single malt, Harry seemed to relax a little and began to talk about himself and his family, and Josh found himself warming to this tall, slim, obviously intelligent, long-haired young man.

Thus they planned a very pleasant weekend to celebrate Josh's retirement, with a day at York Races, a meal at the Horse & Farrier, and Harry pleased Josh by opting to sleep downstairs on the sofa.

The following morning, they set off for York. Josh had given each of them one hundred pounds from his retirement fund, the agreement from the previous evening being that they would bet twenty pounds on each of the five races, and that evening they would explain their tactics for betting, and whoever had won the most, would buy the first drink that evening, and if they had won enough, the evening meal would be on that person. They had a wonderful day out and a few drinks each, with the exception of Beverley who had opted to drive.

That evening, Holly had to buy the drinks and meals, it was time for explanations.

Beverley went first and said that she had known some of the police officers at the meeting who had access to the jockeys and stable hands who had been giving tips. She had faithfully followed those tips and had won fifty pounds on one race but had left the races fifty pounds down.

Harry said that he had been more scientific and knowing that they were going to the races, in advance, had studied form as best he was able in the week before the event and had won forty-five pounds on one race, leaving with a deficit of fifty-five pounds.

Josh said that he had simply placed twenty pounds on the favourite of each race and had lost the lot.

Holly said that she had taken a newspaper and closed her eyes and had stuck a pin in the paper, betting on whichever horse's name the pin landed on. She said that she was delighted to pay for the drinks and meals as she left the races with three hundred and fifty pounds in her purse.

Josh insisted that she keep the money, and they had a splendid meal, which he was happy to pay for and to delight in the company he was in.

Chapter Six

The following Monday, his daughters and Harry having returned to their duties, Delany started work at Pasternak Solicitors, where his new boss, a jovial character named Jim Jameson, said,

'We'll break you in gently.'

'No problem,' said Delany, 'throw me in at the deep end.'

'OK, your first job is a man called Jimmy Savage. He's forty-five years old and lives on the Brompton Estate, he has made claims in the past prior to this claim and he was on a good sickness pension following his claim for an injury after a dodgy road traffic accident, a minor bump at a roundabout.

'However, this claim is a big one. He stepped into the road in front of an apparently slow-moving car, the driver, we believe, had just set off from the side of the road.

'Savage says the driver was speeding and knocked him high into the air and sent him crashing to the ground. The driver says he was barely moving, twenty miles per hour at most, and merely brushed against Savage, who simply fell over.

'There are no other witnesses. He says that he is now paralysed from the waist down. He has made the claim for a quarter of a million pounds through Chapel Solicitors down on the High Street. See if you can find the truth for us.'

Delany decided that he would start off by having a look at Savages address, 45 Brompton Court. He found the address to be a small, council-owned terraced town house on the Brompton estate. The house was reasonably tidy-looking with a short drive and a modern four-wheel drive car parked outside.

He decided to wait and see what happened. After about an hour, the door opened and a chubby woman pushed a wheelchair bearing a similar-looking chubby man through and towards the car. He looked old for a forty-five-year-old having gone bald and was prematurely grey.

Delany watched with interest, knowing that the man must weigh around twenty stones. He had been issued with a camera, by Jameson, which he got ready. The car was obviously custom-built for wheelchairs and the woman opened the back, dropped down a ramp and pushed the chair inside with what appeared to be practiced skill. She wound him up with the mechanism and closed the car door.

Delany followed them to their destination, which was a public house. After ten minutes, he followed them in. It was a late Monday afternoon, and the pub was quite crowded. He took out a newspaper and sat, doing a crossword whilst quietly watching Savage. About one hour later, while his wife was at the bar, Savage suddenly wheeled his chair in the direction of the public toilets.

Delany followed, and there was no one else about, and as Savage got to the gent's toilet door, Delany ducked into the doorway of the ladies' just as Savage wheeled himself right up to the toilet door, raised his right foot and tried to push it open. He was clearly struggling, the chair was too wide for the doorway.

Savage looked around and could see no one watching. He got out of the chair, left it in the corridor and walked into the toilet, apparently, without any difficulty.

'Ah, me thinks the man's a cheat,' said Delany to himself.

He gave Savage a couple of minutes, then followed him in. The toilet was a large room, with several urinals and five stalls with lockable doors.

In case Savage had heard him enter, he began to whistle and noisily use the urinal. He then opened and closed the door to the corridor, remaining quietly inside and setting his camera on movie mode.

Savage came out of the cubicle, completely unaware, he did not see Delany, who had pressed himself into a corner, and he casually walked across to the sink to wash his hands. As he turned back towards the door, he suddenly saw Delany, 'What the f…'

Delany merely smiled and said 'Ah, 'tis another miracle', switched off his camera and walked out of the pub, back to his car, thinking to himself, *I wonder if they are all going to be that easy.*

Jameson was delighted on Delany's return to the office. However, Delany's next few jobs were pretty routine, taking statements from claimants and witnesses, photographs of potholes in the roads, cracked and damaged pavements, staircases which needed improvement, all the things people regularly made insurance claims about and most of which he recommended payment. He noted that the solicitors accepted his recommendations in all these matters.

Two weeks later, he was called into Jameson's office. 'We've got a slightly dodgy one here, this bloke's apparently died in an accident at sea a couple of months ago, having taken out a life insurance policy just three months before that for one million pounds. His wife has applied for a death certificate and an insurance payout, which, of course, means that if she is granted the certificate, she is likely to have a valid insurance claim. Because of the proximity of the dates, we need to have a look at it.'

Delany read the file, which stated that Jack Drummer was the owner of a yacht. He had taken the yacht out to sail off the Northern French coast and visit some of the French ports and had never returned; although, parts of what had been identified as the boat had been found by local fishermen in the Solent following a ferocious storm in that area two days before.

His body was never found, and it was assumed he had perished. Delany remembered seeing the report on the television news at the time.

Delany thought, *Pretty straightforward. Surely, it's a valid claim; however, take a look at it I will.*

He visited the home of Drummer's wife, Marjory, a pretty blonde woman in her forties, and found her to be co-operative, if a little weepy when speaking of her husband.

Her sister and brother-in-law, Joan and Philip Makinson, were visiting at the time. Philip Makinson was a large chubby man, with black hair and a pudgy thick-lipped face. Mrs Drummer related the story to Delany just as he had read it in the reports. Jack had gone for a lone sale around the French coast where he liked to call in at various French ports. And as he left the English shores, he had, apparently, run into a mighty storm and had not been seen since.

'Where did Jack work?' he asked her.

'He was a self-employed writer doing bits for local newspapers. He occasionally got an item in the nationals.'

Delany, feeling that there was nothing more to gain, gave her his card and returned to the office, where he verified that there had been a storm at that time, it left him still thinking that the claim looked genuine.

A few days later, he received a telephone call from Philip Makinson, who said that he would like a meeting away from his wife and her sister. Delany arranged to meet him in a bar in town. When they met, Delany bought him a beer, and they sat together in a corner of the bar.

'What can I do for you?' Delany enquired.

'It's more what I can do for you.'

Makinson handed to Delany a passport. He saw that it related to Jack Drummer.

'Don't you think', said Makinson, 'that if you were sailing around France, you would take this with you?'

'I do indeed, how did you get that?' questioned Delany.

'I was suspicious, it was something she said, and I looked for it in their bedroom the last time we visited when I pretended to go to the toilet. Just before he sailed from England, Jack had been ill with flu symptoms, and as I understood it, he had decided not to go on this particular trip; if he went, he changed his mind on the very last minute. I can also tell you that around that time, my passport disappeared from a drawer in my home. I have since applied for a replacement.'

'Could he have taken your passport?'

'No, I don't think so, but Marjory could have. She is at our house a lot, we just keep our passports in a drawer in our bedroom. The toilet is upstairs, so she could have taken it anytime.'

'Right, I'm trying to understand the implications of what you are telling me. Are you and Jack similar in appearance?'

'Almost identical, people often say they can't tell us apart; here, I have brought a recent photograph of Jack.' He handed it to Delany, who saw immediately the likeness between the two.

'Why are you telling me all this?'

'If Jack is alive and using my identity somewhere in the world, I don't want his sins, past, present or future, to come visiting me at my door.'

'If he is alive and I came across him, how could I be certain that it is him? Has he got any identifying features unique to him?'

'He has a heart tattoo with the name Marjory on his left shoulder, that's all I can think of. Listen, I don't want my wife or her sister to know I have been talking to you, OK?'

Later that day, Delany spoke to an old work colleague, a man who owed him a few favours and was currently working at Manchester Airport, and asked if anyone by the name of Philip Makinson had travelled from Manchester around the time of the report into the yacht disaster.

Two days later, he received a call from the officer, who said that Philip Makinson had travelled from the airport the day following the news report to Cyprus, he could find no record of any return to Manchester by Makinson.

He rang Makinson, apologising for the intrusion. 'Has Jack Drummer any affiliation with Cyprus that you know of?'

'Yes, he was in the army there twenty years ago. He's mentioned opening a bar there one day.'

'Thanks,' said Delany, and rang off, thinking, *I was in the army in Cyprus, but sometime later, I don't remember Drummer.*

Delany related the facts to Jameson.

'So what are you suggesting, that we fund you on a jolly to Cyprus in the hope of finding Drummer?'

'Unless you can think of anything better, the alternative is paying off the insurance claim either now or in seven years, a claim which, on the face of it, now looks to be fraudulent.'

'Good grief,' Jameson said, with mock sincerity, 'You've only worked for us for five minutes and we're sending you off on a free holiday.'

One week later, Delany arrived at Larnaca International Airport and made his way by taxi to Limassol, where he booked in at the Hotel Kikkos.

The following morning, he made his way to the British Army base at Akrotiri where he had previously served and had indeed spent some of the last days of army service. He wondered if any of his old colleagues were still serving there.

He approached the sentry on the gate and introduced himself, it seemed that his fame from those far-off days was still alive, as he was received warmly by the gate guard. He asked if anyone was still in service from those days, fifteen years ago, and was told that Sergeant Major John Stevens was probably the only one who had been around then.

'Good heavens,' said Delany, 'He was but a youth then, and now he's your Sergeant Major. Wow.'

Ten minutes later, after a phone call from the guard, a large red-faced man, in his forties, approached the gate. 'Bloody hell, it's Josh Delany, not seen you for many a long year, believe you're in the cops now. Come on in, let's have a couple of drinks for old times' sake.'

The couple of drinks turned into several, and both men enjoyed their reunion greatly. Delany told Stevens the reason for his visit to Cyprus and gave Stevens a copy of Drummer's photograph; he promised to help where he could.

Back at his hotel, Josh faced the realities of his undertaking. Cyprus was a big island, with several cities and many small towns and villages, how was he going to find Jack Drummer, alias Philip Makinson, who had now, no doubt, changed his appearance and probably his name as well for a second time. His employers had only sanctioned a one-week stay, it seemed an impossible task.

He started in Limassol, going around hotels, showing the photo to desk clerks and hotel staff. He contacted local police officer, members of the International Police Association, who were friendly and well disposed towards him as a retired member of that organisation but were unable to help with his quest.

Not deterred, he travelled to Ayia Napa and Nicosia until he was sick of walking into hotels and pestering staff. The evenings, however, he decided to keep to himself, sitting on his balcony overlooking the Mediterranean, sipping good red wine and reading one of his favourite authors.

The morning of his last day in Cyprus soon came around, and he knew he faced failure. He caught a taxi to Paphos, where he had decided to spend his last day, searching for Drummer.

As the taxi approached Paphos on the top side of the town and began to turn left towards the beach, Delany was gazing idly through the window when he saw a woman he thought he recognised walking down the hill towards the beach. He shouted to the driver, 'I'll get out here.'

He took his time getting out of the vehicle, allowing the woman to walk past down the hill. He paid off the driver, got out of the car, put on his sunglasses and hat and began to follow the woman, who, he saw, was carrying a beach bag, until he could get a better look at her.

As she got to the beach area, she turned left, walking past the many cafés until she came to one, entered and sat, waiting for service.

As he walked past with his sun hat pulled down over his face, he looked at her and saw that he was correct, she was

Marjory Drummer. Fortunately, she did not look his way, and he entered a café further along from where he could see her.

After about thirty minutes, she was joined at her table by a man, a slim-built man, with light brown hair and a greying beard, wearing a t-shirt and shorts. Drummer, he recalled from the photograph, was a stocky man, with dark hair, clean shaven, with a pudgy face. Could this man be a disguised Drummer? He could not know from his appearance. He remembered the tattoo mentioned by Makinson, 'Has he had the foresight to have had it removed?' he said to himself.

After the couple had wined and dined, they paid their bill and walked off towards the beach, followed by Delany. They took up a couple of side-by-side loungers under a parasol and settled down to read.

Delany took a lounger two rows back from them and waited. Eventually, the man took off his shirt, settled down and appeared to fall asleep.

From Delany's position, he could see a dark mark on the man's left shoulder. He waited for about twenty minutes until he was sure the man was sleeping, then set his camera on movie mode and quietly approached them from behind, he focused on the tattoo, on which he saw clearly the word "Marjory". He moved the camera around the couple to take in their whole bodies, then their faces, at which Marjory Drummer opened her eyes.

She shouted, 'What on earth are you doing?'

Delany carried on filming, took off his sunglasses and hat and said, 'Do you remember me, Marjory?'

'Oh my god!' she shouted, 'It's the bloody insurance agent.'

Drummer woke, 'What the?'

'It's that bloody agent I told you about,' screamed Marjory Drummer.

Her husband was now wide awake. 'Look, mate, there's a few grand in this for you. Just destroy that film, forget you've seen me, ten grand when the insurance pays out.'

Delany walked away as quickly as he could, he heard Drummer behind him shout, 'Twenty grand.' He jogged towards the taxi rank at the bottom of the hill.

Before he could climb into the front cab, the Drummers caught up with him. Jack Drummer grabbed him by the shirt front and shouted, 'Fifty grand.' Delany pushed the camera into its case and slung it over his shoulder.

Marjory Drummer came up from behind him, she took hold of the camera case and yanked it from his shoulder, shouting 'Come on, Jack, I've got his camera', and they both ran off in the opposite direction. Marjory shouted, 'He's got nothing now Jack.'

Delany got into the cab and directed the driver to his hotel in Limassol. The driver said, 'They stole your camera, do you want the police.'

Delany said, 'No thanks, mate,' he settled back in his seat and smiled, patting the top pocket of his shirt and felt the SIM card nestling against his chest.

On the way, he said to the taxi driver, 'Wow, how lucky can you get.'

The driver said, 'Eh.'

Delany said, 'Nothing mate,' and gave him a generous tip at the end of the journey.

That evening, he had a farewell drink with John Stevens, who apologised for his inability to help him with his task. Delany said, 'No problem. He had changed his appearance so much that I could have easily walked past him in the street without recognising him. I was just lucky to spot his wife.'

Two days later, he found himself in Jameson's office, discussing the matter.

Jameson said, 'A damn good job, you've saved the firm a small fortune. The police can take over from there. I suspect he's got a few years' jail time to come. You've got a five grand bonus coming, by the way.'

Delany said, tongue in cheek, 'Is that the best you can offer? The other party offered me fifty grand.'

'Take it or leave it,' laughed Jameson.

'I'll take it.'

He decided to blow the five thousand on a long weekend in Paris with his daughters and Harry, the latter of whom Delany was now very fond. He booked them into a small but decent hotel just off the Champs-Elysees.

The March weather was excellent, and they enjoyed a wonderful two days, eating first-class French food, drinking excellent wine and visiting many tourist attractions, including The Louvre, Notre Dame De Paris, The Sacre-Coeur, The Arc De Triomphe and taking the full journey to the top of the Eiffel Tower.

Chapter Seven

Back at work, Josh soon got into the routine of his job. He began to realise that investigations like the Drummers were few and far between, so he just got stuck into the routine and time passed.

After work, one evening, he sat down to watch a local news report on television, not aware that for the second time in his life, his heart was about to be broken again and his life about to change dramatically.

A breaking news flash came into focus, showing a block of flats with small balconies four storeys high. The reporter, a woman, said, 'A man's body was found at the foot of the flats in Manchester, early this morning. He has not yet been identified, it is not known yet if foul play was involved, and some of the flats are known to be occupied by students from Manchester University.' She gave a telephone number for the information bureau for anyone who may be concerned.

Delany rang the number immediately and found it to be engaged. In frustration, he rang the number several time during the next half hour, which seemed to him to be much longer, until, eventually, he received a reply. He was told the name of the flats, Holbrook House, which confirmed his worst fears that it was his daughter's address.

'Has there been an incident room set up yet?' he asked.

'Sort of,' came the reply, 'It's a caravan just outside the flats.'

'I'll make my way there.'

'No, please don't do that, sir, someone will come to see you.'

'My daughter lives in those flats, I'm on my way.'

The forty five minutes it took Delany to drive to Manchester seemed interminable. He had been to the flats several times before, and as he reached them, he saw the police caravan and decided to go there first rather than his daughter's flat, assuming that she would be at the university at that time of the day.

He looked at his watch and saw it was just after two o'clock in the afternoon. He spoke to the Detective Sergeant in charge, who identified himself as Sergeant Ramwell. Delany explained who he was and that his daughter lived in one of the above flats, he learned that the body had not been discovered until eleven that morning as it was deep in a stairwell below the balconies.

'Has the body been removed yet?' he asked.

'No, Forensics are still examining it in situate,' the sergeant replied.

'Can I see it please? I promise I won't get in the way, and I may be able to help,' he said, hoping that was not the case.

'I don't see why not. We will have to wait until forensics are finished.'

Twenty minutes later, the forensics officer, a young woman, came to the caravan and spoke to the sergeant.

'There's no identification on him. It looks like he died about twelve hours ago. He is extensively injured. Much more than a simple fall into the stairwell, it's much more likely that he has fallen from one of the balconies above. We will need access to those balconies. The body can now be removed.'

Delany and the Sergeant went to view the body. The scene was being guarded by uniformed police officers. As they approached, Delany could see that the body was deep in the stairwell and could not easily have been seen from the street. To say he was extensively injured, was an understatement. It had collided with the handrail leading to the basement with so much force, it had almost been cut in half.

Delany descended the steps so that he was beneath the body and could look up at its face, which was badly bruised. His worst fears were realised. It was indeed Harry Woodstock, his daughter's beloved boyfriend.

Delany had never fainted in his life, but he came close at that moment. Many thoughts flashed through his mind, not the least of which was, *Where is Holly, what has she got to do with this and why has she not reported it?*

When he was able to gather himself together, he shouted to Ramwell, 'Follow me.'

He ran into the flats and up the staircase, to the fourth floor and Holly's flat. As he went, he struggled through his pockets, searching for the key which she had given him only weeks before.

He could hear Ramwell labouring up the three flights behind him, shouting, 'Don't go in.' As he approached the flat, he almost choked on the strong smell of bleach coming from inside. He entered, followed by Ramwell.

Inside the flat, the smell was overpowering, the carpets, walls and furniture were all soaked with what could only be a bleach substance. He called her name, 'Holly', as he ran from room to room, but there was no sign of her. The smell in the bedroom was stronger than ever, he saw that there were no sheets or pillows on the bed which had been stripped down to the mattress. By this stage, Delany was in deep despair.

'She may be at the university,' he said to Ramwell, 'I'll go and find out.'

'No, you won't, you're in no fit state. You come down to the caravan, and I'll get an officer to check for her at the university.'

Ramwell sat Delany down in the caravan and made arrangements to have an officer call at the university. Now that he was fully aware that serious crime was involved, he sent for his boss, Detective Chief Inspector Paula Smithson. He also asked the Scenes of Crime Investigator to check out the flat.

'Anybody I can get for you?' he asked Delany.

'Yes, my other daughter, Beverley, she's a policewoman in Manchester.'

'Yes, I've met her. She's on duty now I think. I'll send for her.'

A short time later, Paula Smithson arrived at the caravan. As she walked into the caravan, she immediately saw Delany sitting in the office. 'Josh, is that you?' she asked. At that, Delany recognised her, despite the passing of almost sixteen years. She had been his Sergeant Instructor at the Police Training College at Bruche Warrington all those years ago. Although Delany was not in any state to be sociable, he noted that she was still a very good-looking woman, and he politely said, 'Hi, Paula, you haven't changed all that much.'

Beverley arrived shortly afterwards, and he took her into one of the side rooms to tell her what had happened. He tried to comfort her as she broke down into floods of tears. It was about this time that news came from the university that Holly had not been seen since the previous day.

Later that day, the Scenes of Crime Officers reported that they had not found any DNA evidence or fingerprints due to the extensive and expert "cleaning" of the flat.

However, scuff marks indicated that the man had fallen, probably by force, from the balcony of that particular flat. It also looked as if he had been severely beaten before the fall. Smithson declared the incident was now a murder investigation.

Beverley invited her father to stay with her at her flat, an offer which he gratefully accepted. That evening, they sat up until the early hours, trying to piece together and make sense of the previous twenty-four hours.

That night, he found sleep impossible for a while, and when he did eventually drift off, he found himself dreaming of events he had not thought of for many years. He was back in South Yemen, with the British Army Training Team fighting the local tribesmen against the Yemeni Guerrillas. Suddenly, his dream switched to Goose Green and the fearsome fighting there. He woke up screaming and pouring with sweat, his immediate thoughts were how the investigation was going.

At the Central Police Station, Paula Smithson was more than ready to talk to him, but the news was not good. Nothing had been found, either on the body of Harry Woodstock or in the flat, to indicate who the offenders were. The flat had not been broken into. The cleaning of the flat had removed all signs of evidence. A full murder enquiry team had been set up, and Paula assured him that she would keep him abreast of any developments. She was under no illusions, someone had gone to great lengths to spoil the scene, and this was going to be a long and difficult investigation.

Delany rang Jameson at the insurance firm and told him that he would be unavailable for the foreseeable future and explained why. Jameson told him to take as long as he wanted, his job with the firm would remain open.

He found himself a small rental near the university and began to drink each evening in local bars and clubs, hoping to hear gossip which would lead somewhere. Some weeks later, he was sitting down to an evening meal at his rental when he heard a knock on the door. He answered.

'Bloody hell, Baldy, what are you doing here.'

'Heard you were in trouble and needed me,' came the reply.

'You heard right, my friend, come in.'

That evening, Delany went through the whole story again with Baldy, leaving nothing out, even though he was unsure how Baldy could help under these circumstances.

'You forget', said Baldy, 'I've spent the best years of my life in Strangeways Prison, only half a mile from here. I probably know most of the old lags in Manchester, and I've a fair idea where most of them drink. I'll have to stay here with you, and you'll have to fund my nightly excursions into the city, and I'll do my best to find something out.'

'You can stay so long as you have a bath now and then and occasionally change your clothes. I can smell you from here.'

'Clothes, that's something else you'll have to fund,' said Baldy.

Rather than Baldy dress up, they decided that Delany would have to dress down if he was to accompany him to some of the pubs and clubs Baldy had in mind.

However, Baldy insisted that he go alone to the places, where he was most likely to gain information, as the presence of a stranger would have the effect of closing mouths. In any case, they could not ask direct questions, they would just have to be content with local gossip.

For the next two days, they went from pub and bar, to pub and bar, having no luck. Not even bumping into anyone known to Baldy. On the third evening, however, Baldy said, 'Look at that guy over there, I'm sure I know him from the old days, he is called Ben Johnson, and some people call him Crabby.' They began a conversation with the man, a slight-built scruffy chap, probably in his sixties, who looked a bit like Baldy. They talked in general about criminal life some twenty and thirty years before.

'Up to anything now?' asked Baldy.

'Nah not much, getting a bit too old, welfare does me nowadays.'

'Anything much going on 'round here?' asked Delany.

'Who is he, Baldy? Asking questions like that, I don't know him.'

'Ah, he's just a mate, a nosey sod, ignore him.'

Back at the lodgings, Baldy turned on Delany, 'Look, you can't go asking direct questions like that to people you don't know, you'll just get on the wrong side of them. I know you're en ex-copper and coppers ask question, but it won't work with these old lags. You're just going to have to leave it to me.'

So Baldy began to go out alone, leaving Delany frustrated at the enforced inactivity. He rang Paula Smithson, who reported no progress. He invited her out for dinner that evening, she accepted, saying, 'I hope that this is not just an opportunity to grill me about progress,' he lied and said that it was not.

He met her at the Metropolis Hotel in the city, and they enjoyed a fine meal accompanied by a generous amount of wine.

'Are you with anyone these days, Paula? Em. A man, I mean?' he said, slightly embarrassed by the question.

'No, I was divorced recently, how about you?'

'My wife died a few years ago,' he said and explained the circumstances, and, of course, omitting his own involvement.

Delany then questioned her closely about progress, or indeed lack of it, on the investigation.

'What about noise?' he said, 'Surely, students in the other flats below and close to Holly's flat would have heard something.'

'We, of course, thought of that. The flats were custom-built as, mainly, student accommodation and the abatement of noise systems were built into the flats at the time. In any case, it was holiday time and a lot of the students were away. We have questioned all the other occupants who were there at the time. Nobody heard a thing.'

At the end of the evening, he at least felt a little better than he had for a while, due to the effects of the wine, the good meal and the company of an attractive woman.

The weeks went by. Baldy reported one night that he had made a little progress. He had found out that there was a drug gang operating and supplying cannabis, cocaine and other drugs to students at the university.

He heard they worked as a cartel with a vague Mr-Big-figure in the background, but he had been unable to get any names at all from anyone.

Delany passed that information on to Paula, who promised to look into that angle of things.

Chapter Eight

A week later, Paula rang Delany, 'Can you come into the office? I want to discuss a matter with you,' she would say no more, so Delany got there as quickly as he could.

On arrival, at Paula's office, he saw that Beverly was there before him and immediately feared the worst.

They were seated in a comfortable semi-circle, and Paula began, 'We have found Holly's body.'

The room went quiet as the tragic news sank in. Even though Delany and his daughter had expected this news to come eventually, it still came as a nasty shock.

Delany was the next to speak. 'OK, we're ready, tell us more.'

'At nine this morning, we searched a section of the Bridgwater Canal near Peter Street, and we found the decomposed body of a young woman wrapped in bedding and weighted down with chains and stones. Because of the state of the body, there was no way of identifying her other than dental records which we had already obtained. There can be no doubt that it is the body of your daughter, Holly.'

Another short silence occurred until Delany said, 'How did she die?'

'From drowning, in the canal water,' answered Smithson.

'So she was alive when she went in.'

'So it seems. There's more I'm afraid, are you ready for this?'

'Please tell us all.'

'Bruising indicates that she had been severely raped, both vaginally and anally.'

'Shit, bastards, they'll pay. Sorry,' said Delany, rubbing his forehead.

Paula said, 'Look, I'll give you time to think and have a cup of tea. I'll come back later.'

Delany turned to his daughter, 'Sorry for the outburst, love, it just came out.'

'Don't worry, dad, I'm with you, they will pay.'

Ten minutes later, Paula came back into the room. Delany said, 'Paula, tell me how you got to know where to look for Holly's body?'

'Josh. I can't tell you that, it came from a protected source.'

'Yes, I get you there. Is Jed Mullins still running the squad?'

'No, he's retired. Superintendent Jerry Saunders has it now, I'm not saying that's where it came from.'

Both of them knew he was referring to the deep cover squad of which he was a one-time member.

'No, 'course not, Paula. I'll take it from here.'

It took Delany a week to arrange a meeting with Saunders, who, even though he knew Delany of old as they had both been under cover at different times in the Manchester area, was very wary and cagey during their meeting.

After the pleasantries, Delany said, 'Look, Jerry, Paula's team knew where to look for my daughter's body, and that information came from somewhere, my guess is that it came from your team. All I want is to speak with that member of your team.'

'Josh. You know from experience that I can't allow that. I have to think about the integrity and safety of my people. You know what it's like out there.'

'Then just give me a name. You know who gave that information, just one name please, and I'll take it from there.'

'I know something of your background; if I give you a name, I must know that I will not be locking you up at some stage in the near future for murder.'

'Jerry, I promise you that I will not kill the person you name or bring you or your department into disrepute in any way.'

'OK. One of my people overheard a conversation, well, more of a drunken boast in a pub from a lad called Eddie McKesson, that he and his mates had dumped a body in the canal near Peter Street. That's all, we didn't know who it was or any more than that. We waited two weeks before we told Paula's team because we did not want any suspicion falling on our operative.'

'But you've not locked him up and questioned him.'

'No. We are very close to a major coup, we won't jeopardize that. He will be questioned eventually, but you know, as well as I do, that he will simply deny all knowledge, and we will have nothing but hearsay.'

'Jerry. Thanks for that. I will be working on it, but I promise you that I won't tread on your toes.'

Chapter Nine

That evening, Delany spoke to his daughter.

'Beverley, I want you to find out all you can about a lad called Eddie McKesson. What his convictions are, if any, who his mates are, anything you can, and please don't say anything about this to anybody.'

Beverley agreed, and they arranged to meet to discuss matters.

A couple of days passed before Beverley got back to him and said that she had found through various intelligence sources that McKesson was a minor part of a threesome of drug dealers who, among other activities, targeted the university and the students quarters.

McKesson, she described as twenty five years of age, flash and outspoken, with a high opinion of himself, given to boasting, the bottom line was that he was not very bright. He had many previous convictions for drug dealing, assault and drunkenness, but the one which took Delany's eye was a previous conviction for rape.

His two gang members included Anthony Baron, who was said to be the boss of the outfit, a nasty piece of work, thought to be responsible for many serious offences, including rape and murder. At six feet five inches, he was very muscular and fit.

Baron had only minor previous criminal convictions for theft and assault, as a juvenile, though he had been tried for the same offence of rape as McKesson and had been found not guilty. Despite all the evidence to the contrary, McKesson had sworn he was not there, and the jury had believed him. He was a regular cage fighter and said to have an overpowering presence and was quick-witted.

Even he had a controller, a person of business who supplied the drugs to him, but at that stage, that person, man or woman, was not named, either because he or she was unknown or because the powers that be were playing their cards very close to their chests.

The third member was Ramsay Simms, described as quiet and sly and two-faced, also a powerfully built man, he had many previous convictions for a variety of offences and had served a prison sentence for offences related to drug dealing and indecent assault. He had also been acquitted from the offence of rape, together with Baron.

'Three very nasty pieces of work,' he said when thanking his daughter for the information.

Delany studied the photographs of all three and placed a call to Baldy. 'I need you again.'

Baldy replied 'OK, but you'll have to pick me up.'

Baldy was, in fact, delighted to be back on the scene, with instructions to find out where these characters hung out and with plenty of Delany's money in his pocket to buy as much booze as his small body could possibly absorb. In fact, he quickly found where the three did their drinking but decided to keep Delany in the dark for a little while to extend his free drinks.

Several days later, he met Delany and informed him that the three were to be seen regularly at Tommy's Bar, a snooker hall not far from the university, where they appeared to have the use of a side room in which they spent a good deal of their time.

Delany said, 'Sorry, Baldy, you're now redundant again,' to which Baldy shrugged his shoulders and said, 'You'll have to take me home.'

The following evening, he again became the old man; he entered Tommy's, bought a pint of local ale and sat quietly in a corner. No one resembling the photograph images entered that evening.

The next evening, he was back and was sipping his second pint when the three entered. They spent an hour or so playing snooker. Another older man entered and went into a side room, followed quickly by the three.

When they came out about twenty minutes later, the older man left immediately. Baron went to the bar, got himself a drink and pointed across at Delany, clearly asking the barman who he was, the barman shook his head.

Baron walked across to him and said, 'Not seen you around here before,' to which Delany replied in his old man voice, 'I've just got a flat 'round the corner, and this seems like a nice place to have a drink.' He hoped that Baron would not ask for an address. Baron appeared to be satisfied and walked away. After all, he was a harmless old man.

Delany decided that it would be a good idea at this point to become something of a regular so that he would be less likely to draw attention to himself. He had heard the expression 'Hide in full view'.

He wanted to get to McKesson on his own but only when he was relaxed and did not suspect that he had any hostile intentions. Delany was a decent snooker player and soon became accepted in the bar.

It was two weeks later when the opportunity came; McKesson came into the hall without his two mates and had clearly been drinking heavily.

Delany asked him if he wanted a game, McKesson said, 'You can't afford to play me.'

'Yes, I can,' said Delany, 'I've just had a big win on the lottery.'

'How much?'

'Whatever you normally play for.'

'No, you dick, how much have you won?'

'Ten grand, how much do you want to play for?'

They had three games at twenty pounds per game, which Delany skilfully lost, and with Delany's help, McKesson was getting very drunk. At the end of the last game, Delany said, 'I don't have another twenty on me, I'll pay you tomorrow night.'

When they had finished playing, they sat together, and Delany was sure at this point that he was reeling McKesson in nicely.

'Where do you keep your money?' McKesson enquired drunkenly.

'In my flat, I just hide it in a drawer.'

'You don't bank it?'

'No, I don't trust banks.'

'Where do you live?'

'In the flats near the university, I'm off up there now.'

'I'll come with you and get my twenty.'

Chapter Ten

Delany set off with McKesson, towards his daughter Holly's former flat. He still had the key and had checked it two days before, and it had not been occupied after her death. It still smelled strongly of bleach and had become notorious among the students, several of whom had refused to live there.

When he had been there previously, he had left a package in the airing cupboard. On the way, he gave McKesson a half bottle of whisky he had laced with a strong sleeping draught. McKesson drank deeply from the bottle and did not notice that he was being assisted to climb the stairs to the flat by the old man.

As they went through the door to the flat, McKesson looked around through a drug- and alcohol-induced haze and slurred, 'I'm sure I've been here before. Where do you keep the money?' He saw in bewilderment that it was completely devoid of any furniture and was clearly trying to say something else as he slumped to the floor, unconscious.

Delany let him sleep for a good while. Searching through his pockets, he found McKesson's cell phone; he scanned the present regular numbers and saw that there were plenty, all in first names or nicknames with the odd exception of one name which jumped out at Delany. This person was the only one listed who had been given the honorific of "Mr" Babcock. Delany wondered why.

McKesson awoke to a splash of water in his face and immediately felt the agony in his limbs, it took a few seconds for him to become aware that he was lying on his back in a bath tub, with his legs tucked under him. He tried to move, to alleviate the pain, but found that he could not. What he could not understand in his fuddled state was that he was completely naked and taped down.

He saw the old man looking at him from above, who said to him, calmly, 'Nothing very nasty is going to happen to you as long as you tell me the truth, do you understand?'

McKesson was practically in tears by this early stage; he nodded, and Delany knew the rest would be easy.

'Do you remember being in this flat before?'

'I don't know where we are,' replied McKesson.

'You recognised the flat when we walked in, it's where you and your mates raped a young girl and threw her boyfriend off the balcony.'

'No, not I, mate.'

'Look, I don't want to use the water on you, tell the truth and you'll be out of here.'

'You got the wrong guy.'

Delany had already filled a jug full of water. He grabbed McKesson by the hair, forced his head backwards and poured the contents over his face. McKesson gurgled, and it took several seconds before he was able to gain a breath, 'OK, I'll tell you, I'll tell you.'

'From the beginning.'

'OK, no more water.'

'We'll see.'

'The girl, she knew we were drug dealing in the flats and threatened to tell the local cops. Tony said that it came from the boss that we had to shut her up. I didn't know what he had in mind, I thought we were just going to threaten her and maybe knock her about a bit, but that's not Tony's way, he wants a lot more than that. He knocked on the door, and she must have thought it was someone else. She opened the door, and we were in.'

'Who's we?'

'Me, Tony and Ramsay, a couple of lads, Sparkler and Flash Johnson, stayed outside and watched the street and corridors.'

'Keep going.'

'If I tell you everything, are you're going to let me go?'

'Certainly. Keep going.'

'Tony said we might as well have a bit of fun, so we ripped her clothes off and took turns with her on the bed. Tony went first, he always does, then me, then Ramsay, but he's a kinky bastard and took her the other way, you know what I mean?'

'What do you mean Tony always goes first, have you done this before?'

'Yea, I've been done for it before, but Tony and Ramsay got away with it. I lied for them.'

'What next?'

'I'm in agony here, let me get up,' he sobbed.

'I will when I've finished; the quicker you tell me what happened, the quicker I will let you get up.'

'Then a bloke, who had a key, came to the door. Sparkler or Flash grabbed him and pushed him in, then went out again. The bloke must have seen what was going on, so Tony grabbed hold of him, he a strong bastard, I think Ramsay was on the girl at the time.'

'What do you mean on the girl, do you mean he was raping her at the time?'

Giving her one, yea, she was screaming and crying, you know how they do.'

Delany stepped back and took a couple of deep breaths, he knew exactly what they had done to his daughter, but to hear it so graphically, hit him in the gut, he almost had tears in his eyes when he went back to McKesson and said, 'Go on.'

'The bloke was shouting and had a go at Tony, tried to hit him, but he had no chance. Tony just gave him a good smacking and made him watch; believe it or not, the bloke started crying as well. Tony said something like "shut your gob you wimp", then pushed him out onto the balcony. He came back in and said something like "he's gone over, clumsy me".'

Delany felt such hatred for this man at this stage that he could happily have throttled him to death there and then, but he knew that would not only be breaking a promise, but that it would not suit the plan he had formulated in his mind.

McKesson said, as evenly as he could,

'Who are you, are you one of Frankie Maxwell's boys? You know what this was about and why we had to do it, don't you? She was in a right state by then, screaming and shouting, it's a good thing these flats are soundproof. We couldn't take her outside like that and couldn't leave her there with all our evidence on her, so we laced her with Ket until she was out of it, took her wrapped in her bed covers and threw her in the canal.'

'Still alive?'

'Yea, I guess so, not for long though, eh?' he tried to snigger but was in too much pain.

At that point, Delany almost lost his cool. He swayed with rage, he wanted to tear McKesson to pieces, but knew he had to keep his cool if his plan was to work. He continued,

'Who cleaned the flat?'

'Someone Tony knows, a copper I think. Summat to do with the cop's anyway.'

'Last question, then you can go. Who's Mr Babcock?'

'Don't know any Mr Babcock.'

Delany filled the water jug from the tap above McKesson's head.

'OK, I'll tell you. Mr Babcock is our boss, everybody thinks that's Tony, but it's not. He supplies our gear and takes most of the profit, he's the one who had the flat cleaned.'

'Does he go in Tommy's Bar? I've seen an older man in there with you.'

'Go in? He owns the bar. He is Tommy; he owns lots of bars around Manchester.'

'Where does he get his gear?'

'Amsterdam, it comes in once a week.'

'When is the next one due?'

'Oh, come on, I can't tell you that.'

Delany poured the water, McKesson choked and gagged for breath.

This time, it took McKesson a couple of minutes to recover. When he did, he gabbled as though he could not get it out quickly enough, 'All right, I'll tell you, the next is due tomorrow afternoon, back of Tommy's. Comes in during the afternoon, warehouse, under the railway arches two blocks from Tommy's, about three o'clock. Could be any vehicle, usually a car, and gears hidden in the tyres.'

'What day is tomorrow?'

'Wednesday of course.'

Delany then realised that McKesson's body clock was a day out as he had slept much of the night, it was now eight on Wednesday morning.

'And that's the day it comes in?'

'Yea, like I said.'

'Listen, I'm going to do you a favour now, even though you don't deserve it. When you leave here, go to the police station and see Detective Chief Inspector Smithson and tell her everything you have told me. Everything, I mean it. You'll do your time for rape and murder. I'll give you two days to do what I say. If you do that, you'll get rid of my shadow. It really will be better for you in the long run.'

'You're bloody joking; you're a cop, aren't you? What I've said, I've said under torture. You will never get away with it in court. They'll bloody laugh at you.'

'By the way, what did the two Johnson boys do?'

'Nowt, they're just doormen Tommy uses.'

'Drink this,' said Delany, forcing the drugged whisky into McKesson's mouth. He had little choice and was soon sleeping soundly. Delany dragged him out of the bath and laid him on the floor, leaving his arms and legs taped up. He would dearly, at that stage, have been happy to choke the life out of McKesson, but he had made a pledge to Saunders and intended to keep faith.

He rang Jerry Saunders, who he thought would be in his office at this time, and, indeed, he was. 'Jerry, it's Josh Delany. I have some information for you,' he related what he had learnt from McKesson about the imminent drug delivery without telling him how he had come by that information, even though Saunders said, 'How do you know all this, can I be sure it's good information?'

Delany replied, 'You will just have to take my word for it. Listen, I need to know immediately that you will resolve this and the outcome.' Saunders promised that he would set up surveillance and inform Delany of the result.

He knew that he had hours to wait and could not free McKesson until later that day. He took a sleeping bag from his pack and settled down to a light sleep a few yards from McKesson who was snoring gently.

He awoke with a start at 4pm that day, looked across and saw that McKesson was still asleep. He then realised that it was his mobile phone which had awoken him. He answered, it was Saunders. 'I don't know how you did it, Josh, but your information was spot on. We have recovered several hundred thousand pounds worth of cocaine and arrested the two couriers and one of a local gang who was there to receive the stuff.'

'Who was the local lad?'

'A lad called Ramsay Simms, why?'

'Oh, just curious. Well done, Jeff. You owe me a pint sometime.'

Delany cut the tapes binding the still-sleeping McKesson, collected his gear and left to return to his lodgings.

McKesson woke about eight that evening, he lay for a moment and recent events began to play back to him in his still-befuddled mind. He realised that he was lying naked on a wet carpet and began to shiver with cold and fear as the memory of what he had told the old man crept in. He had to do something about it.

He dressed quickly and walked to the snooker bar. On arrival, he was met by Baron.

'Where the hell have you been? All hell's let loose here, the cops have raided the warehouse, got all the new gear and Ramsay's been locked up. The boss is going bloody mad, how in hell the cop's got the info; hope, for your sake, it's nothing to do with you.'

''Course it's bloody not, first I've heard of it,' replied McKesson, with even more fear creeping into his heart.

Chapter Eleven

Simms was seated in the interview room at the Central Police Station, alongside the duty solicitor and facing Detective Sergeant Ramwell, who switched on the recorder and cautioned him.

'I'm saying nowt until Mr Salmon is here, he's my solicitor.'

The duty solicitor nodded his acquiescence, and the sergeant dutifully switched off the tape recorder.

Later that day in the interview room, Simms was interviewed by Salmon.

'Ramsay I've looked at the evidence against you. You've no chance of getting off with this one; the two lads who brought the drugs from Amsterdam have coughed up and implicated you. All I can advise you to do is play the game. You say nothing during the interview on my advice so that they can't hold that against you later in court. You plead not guilty at the magistrates' and again at the preliminary hearing at the Crown Court. That means you will wait a few months on remand before your trial. Remand is going to be much easier on you than prison, you'll get a lot more perks. Then, when the trial date arrives, you plead guilty. Your time on remand will count against your sentence and, in any case, the judge then has to give you a more lenient sentence because of your guilty plea, and you win all around.

Back at his lodgings, Delany rang Paula Smithson and invited her out to dinner two evenings hence. She readily accepted, saying, 'I've just heard about the drug bust; well done, you'll have to tell me all about it when we meet.'

They met and had a very pleasant evening and a wonderful meal at the Midlands Hotel. Paula unsuccessfully tried to get information out of Delany, who was not forthcoming, although he found himself becoming very attracted to Paula.

At one point, he said to her, 'Has any member of the public approached you about the death of my daughter?'

'No why do you ask?'

'Oh, just curious.'

'Oh, by the way,' she said, 'Simms has pleaded not guilty, he's probably playing the game that some of them do, he knows that he's bang to rights.'

He spent that night with Paula at her flat, fully aware that this was the first time he had spent a night with a woman since the death of his wife.

The following day, he got out his tape recorder and played the recording he had made of his conversation with McKesson and selected the piece where McKesson said 'the next is due in tomorrow afternoon, back of Tommy's. Comes in during the afternoon, warehouse, under the railway arches two blocks from Tommy's, about three o'clock. Could be any vehicle, usually a car, and gears hidden in the tyres.'

He isolated that piece, then travelled several miles from his lodging and found a suitable telephone box where he rang Babcock's landline which he had retrieved from McKesson's phone, hoping that he would not be available to answer.

He was lucky, and as the phone changed to answer phone, Delany simply played the recorded message into the mouthpiece and rang off.

The following morning, Babcock called Baron, 'Tony, I want you here as soon as you can, urgent business.'

On arrival, Baron found Babcock incandescent with rage. 'Listen to this,' he shouted and played the recording to Baron.

'Who the bloody hell is that?'

'It's Eddie McKesson, I'm certain of that. It's not like him, there must be more to it than meets the eye. Don't worry, boss, I'll get to the bottom of it and find out why he's grassed us up like that.'

'OK, find out why if you can, but you know what the bottom line is, he's no use to us now. He's a total liability.'

Delany decided that it was time to go home as he knew the old man could not appear again. He needed to plan his next moves and to await the outcome of his actions so far.

In fact, it was only three days later when a television news bulletin told him that the mutilated body of a man had been found in a street in Manchester. The murder was believed to have been drug-gang related. A later news report confirmed that the man was Eddie McKesson.

Chapter Twelve

He decided that part one of his plan was complete and that before he started with the next phase, he had to change his appearance completely; in any case, a holiday in the sun would not go amiss. Before he went, he looked up the telephone number of Tony Baron which he had taken from McKesson's cell phone. He rang it from the box he had used previously, there was no reply. Covering the mouthpiece with his handkerchief and disguising his voice, he spoke to the answerphone.

'Baron, this is a warning, take it seriously, go to the police and admit your part in the murder of Harry Woodstock and the rape and murder of Holly Delany. Get rid of my shadow, it will be in your best interests.'

He did it more in the hope of justice than the expectation of success.

Baron reported back to Babcock, 'McKesson finally admitted that it was him who grassed us up, it took a hell of a lot of getting that out of him. He said that he was tortured by an old guy who had recently become a regular at the club. It's hard to believe, but he stuck to the story. I've seen that old guy, and he looked like a harmless old sod to me. He took McKesson back to the flat we had cleaned up and got the info there. McKesson said that the guy's main interest seemed to be the rape and killing of the two at the flat. You remember the two who said they would turn us in to the cops, the two we got rid of? Strangely enough, I've had an anonymous phone call from somebody telling me to admit my part in the stuff that went on in that flat.'

Babcock said, 'Sounds like some undercover rogue cop, we'll need to be careful for a while, you did the right thing getting rid of McKesson. He was a danger to us, keep your head down for a bit and we'll see what happens.'

Delany decided that if he was to go into the next phase, he needed to be as fit as possible, given his age. Two weeks in Madeira would not go amiss at this stage. He made the arrangements, and before he knew it, he was in the capital Funchal, running in the mountains and swimming mile after mile in the hotel pool and the warm seas around the coast.

Two weeks later, Delany was back at home. He had gone unshaven since his date with Paula Smithson and his natural salt and pepper hair and short beard were now well trimmed and jet black. He was now darkly tanned and looked ten years younger than his real age.

He returned to Manchester and decided to look in at Tommy's; number one, to test his new look, and number two, to see how that land was lying after the death of McKesson. He was delighted not to be recognised even by people he had previously played snooker with. On his second visit, he saw Baron drinking at the bar. He ordered a drink himself, and as he expected, Baron was clearly inspecting this newcomer.

He walked across to Delany and said, 'Not seen you here before.'

'No, just in town on a contract,' Delany replied.

'What do you do?'

'Electrical work at some of the local stores, in town for a month or two. This seems like a good place to drink and have a game of snooker,' Delany replied, hoping that Baron knew nothing about electronics.

'Don't cause me any trouble; believe me, you'll be sorry if you do.'

'Sorry, why would I cause you any trouble? I'm just here for the beer and the snooker.'

Baron wandered away apparently satisfied, Delany sighed with relief, it seemed that he had passed the simple test for now. However, while talking to Baron, he saw once more how big, fit, awesome and suspicious this man was and that if he started to watch Baron's movements locally, he would soon bring further unhealthy suspicion down upon himself.

He had heard that Baron was a local cage fighter, so he decided that if he was to assess the opposition adequately, he had better watch him fight.

A week later, Delany was in the audience at a cage fighting competition. He had never witnessed one before and, even with his vast experience of violence, was surprised by the viciousness of it. He watched several fights until it came to the last bout on the agenda. As Baron walked to the cage, he could see exactly what a brute he was, he had known that Baron was a big muscular man, now he saw just how so. *He's got muscles on his pimples,* thought Delany. *How on earth am I going to deal with this brute of a man?*

His opponent entered the cage and Delany saw that he was of similar stature but not so muscular. The ensuing fight was no real contest; Baron simply smashed the other man all over the cage, it ended fairly quickly with the other fighter being carried from the cage, probably to the nearest infirmary, thought Delany.

Baron walked from the cage totally unbruised, hardly sweating as though he was walking away from a pleasant picnic in the countryside. People in the crowd were not happy, booing as the inferior fighter was taken away.

Delany called for Baldy, who was delighted to be called into action once more. Delany asked him to monitor Baron's daily habitual movements without attracting attention to himself. Baldy knew exactly what was wanted and, as usual, took his time getting the information whilst enjoying the extra money in his pockets and the good booze and food, plus the freedom of being away from his wife for a while.

Again, Baldy took his time in weighing up Baron and his movements, eventually reporting to Delany two weeks later.

'You know he's very fit, that's obvious. Word has it, from my local contacts, that he killed McKesson personally. No doubt under orders from Babcock. His routine seems to be regular iron pumping in one of the local gyms, he also runs twice, sometimes three times a week, up through Trafford Park, then along the canal bank at Castle field and Salford Quays, five or six miles on each occasion. He's a monster and weighs around eighteen stones. What are you, five feet nine and ten or eleven stones wet through? You'd be mad to take him on physically, he'll murder you.'

'Leave that to me, you've done your job, now you can go home.'

'I'm going to hang about a while, make sure you don't get into too much trouble.'

'If you're sticking around, you can find out for me what days he goes running.'

The following day, with his next phase plan firmly in his mind, Delany started a fitness programme of his own; he went out running, trying to stay with the routes Baldy had described; on one of his runs, he saw a police car being driven towards him. As it got close, he could see that his daughter, Beverley, was in the passenger seat. This is a good test for my disguise, he thought, the car passed without any look of recognition from his daughter. *Wow, it looks like I've passed the test,* he thought.

That evening, Beverley rang on his mobile, 'Dad, what on earth are you up to? Don't think for a moment I didn't see you today.'

'I'll explain when I see you, please don't worry about me.'

'I know you too well to worry; whatever it is, please be careful.'

Later that day, he went to the local swimming baths to test his endurance, he found that he could swim breaststroke and crawl on the surface for mile after mile, but his underwater endurance was limited to three quarters of the twenty-five-metre length of the pool. *That has to change,* he thought.

Delany went to the baths day after day, week after week, for the next month until he could comfortably complete two and a half lengths of the bath underwater. He knew at that stage that he was in supreme physical condition for his age and was ready.

Baldy, who was aware of Delany's fitness regime, reported to Delany on Baron's general routine, he was particularly interested in his movements whilst out for his regular runs.

'He varies the times and days of his runs with the exception of Monday morning. He always turns out from his flat at six on Mondays and follows the route I've already given you without fail. What's your plan?'

'I've not fully made my mind up yet; you've done enough, you can go home now.'

'I told you I'm sticking around.'

Delany began to run regularly, using the route taken by Baron, particularly on Monday mornings, all the time watching out for Baron. He knew that Baldy was right and that Baron was meticulous about his Monday run, always turning out at the same time and always taking the same route.

He also found that Baron was not a particularly fast runner and that he could easily outpace him whenever he wanted. Whenever he passed Baron in either direction, he did not acknowledge him, and Baron completely ignored Delany.

As he ran by the canal side, Delany spotted a narrow side lane leading down to the canal at an oblique angle. It was six thirty in the morning, and the area was secluded away from the buildings and completely deserted.

The following Monday, he stood at the top of this lane at the same time and waited for Baron to pass. He came by at exactly 7am, and as he came in sight, Delany counted the seconds until he reached the bottom of the lane. Ten seconds exactly. Delany took up different positions on the lane until he found the spot that at his best speed the lane met the tow path exactly ten seconds later.

Eventually one Sunday afternoon, he was with Baldy in one of the local public houses when Baldy said, 'What's going on? You're obviously going to do something, but what and when? You're making me very nervous.'

Delany replied sharply, 'Look, Baldy, none of what is going to happen is anything to do with you, why on earth don't you go home and get the hell out of here?'

For a moment, Baldy was startled by his tone, then he could tell that Delany was also very nervous and that whatever he was going to do was imminent.

That evening, Delany knew that there was a local cage fight and, from pub-gossip, also knew that Baron was fighting and that because of previous public dissatisfaction, he was facing a much tougher and more experienced opponent.

He attended the fight, and as before, Baron's was the final fight. This time, however, the other man looked like he knew his business. The fight went to full term, each man smashing, kicking and gouging the other with great fury.

Baron was given the verdict, but this time, as he left the cage, he was pouring with sweat and covered in bruises. He was elated at winning but clearly knew he had been in a frenzied and close-run fight.

Back at his lodgings, Delany mused that if ever there was a time to tackle Baron, it was now or never.

The following morning, Delany left his lodgings at 6am, it was still dark, and he was in his running gear and walked to the spot on the lane he had previously marked out, and he waited. He felt nervous, slightly afraid but invigorated.

As he left, Baldy heard the door close, and he sat up in his bed. He was fully dressed, he followed Delany, not directly behind, he knew if he did that, Delany would spot him; in any case, he had a rough idea of where Delany was going, as he had followed him to the spot before.

At 7am, Baron appeared running as usual along the tow path. As he appeared, Delany set off and was soon at full speed. In the exact moment that Baron passed the end of the lane, Delany took a deep breath and leapt at him from slightly behind him and from his left.

Delany wrapped both arms around his neck and his legs around his waist as he hit Baron at such speed that Baron staggered towards the canal, but, showing amazing strength, he quickly recovered and tried to rip Delany from his back. Delany had failed to force Baron into the water and was now struggling with a man of vastly superior strength.

71

Delany was then acutely aware that he had underestimated Baron and that he was about to lose a very uneven contest.

Baldy having correctly guessed what Delany had in mind and having feared that Delany was neither big, nor strong enough to defeat Baron in a straight physical contest. He moved towards the struggle as quickly as he was able, and as he got there, he saw that Delany was about to be savaged by Baron. Baldy ran at the struggling pair from behind, and with all his bodyweight, he shoulder-charged, hurling them into the water and falling in behind them.

A great struggle began, Delany, who was unaware of the presence of Baldy, was soon aware that he had made two big mistakes: the colossal strength and fighting ability of Baron, and the depth of the canal at that point.

At first, the shock of the entry into the water had stunned Baron, and he merely thrashed his arms about until he quickly became aware of his mortal danger. He then gripped Delany's arms and forced them away from his neck, coughing and choking as he scrambled with his feet and was eventually able to stand in the less-than-five-feet-depth and take in a quick and shallow breath.

Baron's feet slipped from under him and he fell backwards onto Delany who was able to regain his grip around Barons neck. The pair rolled over and over. Baron was able to stand again, this time taking a deeper breath; he again forced Delany's arm from his neck, and this time, Delany knew that he was in deep trouble.

He was now fighting a much stronger man on unequal terms. Delany was also able to take a quick breath, though he feared that he was about to lose the fight and, therefore, his life.

The battle went on for several more minutes, with Baron gaining the upper hand; suddenly, and to Delany's delight and relief, Baron pitched forward into the water and Delany was able to re-grip his hold around his opponent's neck.

This time, Baron seemed unable to regain his feet, even though he thrashed around. Delany now felt hope that he was better equipped to win the underwater battle because of his previous conditioning, he knew that Baron was weakening and was now unable to tear Delany's arms from around his neck.

Delany hung on and on, feeling Baron go slack in his grasp but fearing to let go in case he was feigning. At last, he could stay under no longer and surfaced. Baron also surfaced face down, and Delany knew he had won.

Delany stood to leave the canal when to his horror, he saw that there was a third person in the water who was also floating face down. He turned the body over and saw it was Baldy.

'What the bloody hell…' he said, dragging Baldy to the side of the canal and heaving him out and onto his back.

He could not feel a pulse, Baldy's face was purple and he was not breathing. He tilted Baldy's head back, pinched his nose and blew hard into his mouth, all he could hear was water gurgling in Baldy's lungs. Delany pushed him unto his stomach and pushed hard on his back several times until he saw a stream of foul water pour from Baldy's mouth and nose, he beat Baldy hard on the chest, hoping to restart his heart, and he resumed mouth-to-mouth treatment.

Baldy began to cough, splutter and gasp for breath. Delany turned him onto his side and saw the natural colour slowly returning to his face.

A few minutes later, Baldy appeared to return to normality. Delany looked around and breathed a sigh of relief. Baldy was OK and there was no one about. Questions could come later, he got Baldy to his feet, and they set off back to the lodgings.

Back there, Baldy explained he had been apprehensive the evening before when he had seen how nervous Delany had been, he had got up early that morning and followed Delany, although he could not keep up with Delany, he knew roughly where he was going.

He hid in the bushes and saw Delany just as he leapt at Baron and saw the way the fight was going. He knew that Delany was about to lose the struggle and went forward and pushed them both into the canal and fell in himself, when Baron stood and forced Delany's arms from his neck, 'I grabbed

Barons legs and pulled, and you both went down into the water. I held on to his legs to stop him from standing again.'

'Then I tried to stand, but I kept slipping, the next thing I remember is you thumping me and blowing into my mouth. I have to tell you that it was a stupid thing to do, taking on a thug like that who's twenty years younger than you and twice as big and super fit to boot;, if I hadn't been there, he would have killed you; don't ever do anything like that again.'

Delany felt duly chastised and grateful. He also realised that the job was not yet done and, in future, he had to be a little cannier.

In the local paper the next day, there was a small article about a jogger having had an accident near the canal when he had apparently fallen in and drowned. Delany had hoped that he would personally leave no bruises on Baron during their struggle that could indicate a struggle in the water, and it was apparent that he had not done so; in any case, his severe bruising would no doubt be put down to the cage fight, as Delany had previously calculated.

Chapter Thirteen

Both he and Baldy went home. There were still four people left who he held responsible, and they had yet to face his wrath.

He knew that he had to find out more about Tommy Babcock, but he decided that he could leave that job to Baldy. Simms was in prison for some time yet, so he could be left for now. Delany went back to work at Pasternak's.

Jameson was delighted to see him.

'Thought you'd deserted us,' he said, 'Got just the job for you. We've had our heads together with other insurance people in town, and together we find that we have had a glut of whiplash injury compensation claims, seven in total, three of them are ours, the other claims are to the other local insurers. The suspicious thing about them is that they stem from exactly the same circumstances, they all say that they were approaching a roundabout at a quiet time of day when the car in front slammed on the brakes for no reason, even though there was no traffic on the roundabout, they crashed into the back of it, then the car drove off without stopping.

Here are all the claim forms, see what you can make of them.'

'Have you paid out on any of the claims so far?'

'Yes, one of them; at first, we had no reason to be suspicious until they came in one after the other to us and the other insurers, all almost identical. Cartwrights down the road made a payout last week to a man called John Simpson.'

Delany took the forms away to study and found that indeed they were highly suspicious, the same roundabout featured on four of the seven and a second roundabout just over a mile away was the scene of the other three. In every case, the crash took place just after darkness, and an elderly vehicle, worth very little, was used by the claimant in each case.

All the claimants were in their forties. There were no witnesses to any of the crashes. All the vehicles were written off, even though the damage to the front was always minor. No one involved had got the make or registration number of the offending vehicle. In each case, the claim said that the police had been called but did not attend, as initially it was reported as a damage only, not injury accident. The whiplash injuries manifested themselves later.

As he read the files, Jameson walked into his office with an eighth identical claim, saying, 'Each claim is covered by a hospital and doctor's report indicating that the claims may be genuine, we are aware of how easy that particular injury is to fake, but we will have to payout unless you can find a good reason not to, no matter how dodgy we regard their claims.'

Delany studied the claim forms and saw that most of the claimants had a land telephone line besides a mobile number. He decided that his first action would be to check the calls from each land line over the previous four months, since the first of the claims had been made.

Ramsay Simms was sitting on the bed in his cell, muttering to himself about how unfair life was and what he was going to do to the people who got him sent down; he had full breakfast in his belly and was watching daytime television. He had been in prison for three months and knew that he still had a long way to go, when a warder entered his cell, saying, 'Simms, you have a female who wants to see you, do we give her the go ahead or not?'

'Who is she?'

'A woman called Silvia Clark.'

'Don't know her, what does she want?'

'No idea, she looks like a bit of a chancer after a bit of a thrill meeting up with prisoners, we get them here from time to time; your choice, do you want to see her or not?'

Simms, who had not had a single visitor in the time he had been at the prison, said,

'Might as well, it'll break up the boredom.'

The following week at visiting time, Simms was seated at a small table in the visiting room, with other inmates watching people enter, when he saw a slim blonde young woman enter the room. *Wow,* he thought, *I hope she's the one.*

She walked to the officer at the desk in front of the room, and he pointed to Simms. She walked over to him and said, 'I'm Silvia. I hope you don't mind me visiting, can I sit down?'

'Yea, 'course you can, do I know you?'

'Don't you remember me? I've seen you in the club. I always thought you were good-looking. Then I heard you'd been sent down, I was really sad. It's taken all my courage to come and see you.'

They talked about Manchester and the snooker club, and as Simms realised that she did not want anything from him other than his company, he began to relax and enjoy her presence.

At the end of the session, he said, 'Will you visit me again?'

She said, 'Yea if you want me to.'

Chapter Fourteen

Delany sat reading the telephone records in front of him. It was going to be a long job he thought, there were many calls over the four months. He was not certain at first what he was looking for other than any connections between the claimants, which he thought were probably unlikely.

As it happened, it did not take long to find the first connection, the records of Mr and Mrs McGrath showed contact with those of John Simpson, the fourth claimant on the list. As he went through the records, he found that several of the claimants were in contact with each other. *But what does that prove?* he mused, *Only that they knew each other, it added to the suspicion but nothing more, nothing conclusive, nothing that would stand up in court.*

Wait a minute, he thought, *I don't have to prove this to a criminal court, only to a civil one with a lesser standard of proof.* Perhaps this is enough. But he was not happy and continued his scrutiny.

After two hours, Delany spotted one telephone number called by each of the claimants on at least one occasion during the four-month period. Delany thought that there may be some connection there, so he took a risk and called the number.

'Hello. Sunnyside Golf Club, can I help you?' came the reply.

Thinking quickly, Delany said, 'Hello, do you cater for meals for non-members?'

'Oh yes, no problem there, should I book a table?'

Delany booked a table for one the next lunch time. 'See you then,' came the reply.

Delany was enjoying an excellent lunch at the club, it was fairly quiet and the young woman serving him seemed pleasant. He had eaten his soup, and when she served the next course, he said to her,

'I may know some people who are members here, a Mr and Mrs McGrath and a John Simpson.'

'Yes, they are regulars, not in at the moment though, but there's a large party booked in tomorrow night and they will be among them, some kind of celebration, I don't know what.'

'Ah, are you working then?' he said, hoping that she was not.

'No, I just do lunches,' she said, a little taken aback.

Before he left, Delany booked for an evening meal the next day.

He arrived at the club at seven thirty the next evening and again found the dining room quiet, although he could hear laughter elsewhere in the club.

He went to the bar to order a drink and asked the barman the direction to the toilet.

'At the end of that corridor on the right, sir, just past the private room.'

As he passed the private room, he could hear a general hub and laughter from inside but could not make out any particular voices. In the toilet cubicle, the noise from the room seemed even louder, but he still could not make out the gist of any conversation.

I don't suppose they'll invite me in, so I may be wasting my time, he thought as he went back to his table.

He was in the middle of eating a succulent rib eye steak when the loud noise from the private room suddenly stopped, and he could hear a single speaker, though he could not make out what was being said.

Damn, he thought while heading for the toilet, *they could time their speeches better.*

It was obviously a very short speech because he got into the cubicle just in time to hear a male voice saying, 'We have to thank the club secretary for furnishing us with the second of these splendid windfalls and John Simpson for paying for this wonderful repast. We should meet here again next time, and may that be soon.'

Delany managed to finish his dinner before he heard the scraping of chairs from the private room, indicating to him that they were about to leave. He went outside and moved his car across the car park to a position opposite the exit where he could clearly see all the cars as they left.

He counted the people as they came out, seventeen in all. As the cars left the park, he noted that they were all newish, good quality vehicles and took all the registration numbers.

Back at the office, he made a report and forwarded the numbers to the DVLA at Swansea to identify the drivers.

Chapter Fifteen

Simms was receiving his second visit from Silvia and was very pleased that she had come to see him again.

'Hi, wasn't sure I'd see you again.'

'Why not, rough lads like you excite me.'

'You think I'm a rough lad?'

'Yeah, I've heard all sorts of stories about you in Manchester, they reckon you've raped and killed a girl.'

'What the hell, are you some kind of nark or a journalist or something, you're not a copper, are you?'

'Am I? Hell, I just like a bit of rough, it scares me, and I like that.'

'I'm out of here in a few months, are you not scared I might kill you?'

'No, but I wouldn't mind if you knocked me about a bit.'

Wow, thought Simms, *This could get very interesting.*

At the end of the session, he said, 'Will you come and see me next week?'

'Can't see next week, but I'll come as often as I can.'

Delany got the results of the DVLA enquiry and went to see Jameson.

'It's as I thought, all the claimants to you and the other insurers were at the dinner at the golf club. It's obvious now that they were celebrating Simpson's payout and looking forward to others', how much have you paid them so far?'

Jameson said, 'The McGraths got seven and a half grand a month or two back and Simpson got ten grand, it depends on the severity of the neck injury claimed for; anyway, well done, that will do me, there won't be any more payouts.'

'Fine,' said Delany, 'But don't you want your money back from those paid out and maybe a police prosecution?'

'I know you're an ex-copper, Josh, but, no, we're not looking for a prosecution, but, yes, it would be good to get the money back.'

'A prosecution would not only get your money back, it would get into the papers and be a deterrent to others intending to defraud. At the moment, we have got nothing on the man I think is probably the ringleader of the group, I believe that is the club secretary; at the moment, I don't even know his name.'

'Well, there is that, Josh. Go for it.'

Delany had noticed that not only were all the claimants at the golf club dinner, there was also a couple, James and Sophia Ringway, who were not claimants. *Were they the next people to dip their fingers in the pie?* mused Delany.

A check with the records of registered club soon revealed that the secretary was a man called Hugh Bennett and that he lived alone in a small disused farm a few miles outside the city.

He decided to pay the farm a quiet visit, first he called at the club to make sure that Bennett was there.

'Is Mr Bennett there at the moment?'

'Yes, do you want to speak to him?'

'Not at the moment, but I will call in later.'

As the receptionist asked for his name, he rang off.

On arrival at the farm, he noted that it was in a large spread-out area with several outbuildings. It was nine o'clock in the evening and going dark, his excuse if seen was to ask for directions to a local public house, but in any case, the house was in darkness and it was unlikely that anyone was inside.

He tried the doors of the first two outbuildings, they were locked, the third building was an open barn and parked in a corner was an old Land Rover vehicle, the vehicle was well battered and dented all over and had obviously been used for farm work of some kind for many years.

He took out his torch and examined the rear of the vehicle; it did not appear to be any more damaged than any other part. However, there was a large tow bar at the rear, protruding at least eighteen inches, which he saw was damaged and faintly smeared with different-coloured paint tracings. *Not much use those*, he thought, *All the claimants' vehicles have been scrapped, nothing to check this against.*

Delany attended the local police station, where he spoke to Sergeant Thompson who he knew from his previous service.

'Frank. I'm pretty sure that over the next week or so, you will get a call from someone called Ringway, who will report damage only, no injury accident at one of the two roundabouts leading to the city centre. I know that normally you would not attend a minor bump like that, but on this occasion, for reasons, I will explain, I would like you not only to attend, but also to turn out one of the experienced vehicle examiners.'

He went on to give the sergeant the full reason for his request, the name of the suspect, the location of the Land Rover and the likelihood of a serious fraud investigation to follow, if indeed his information was correct. The sergeant, who was young and newly promoted, was eager to do as requested.

Simms was in the visiting room again, looking forward to his visit by Silvia, she was the only one who had visited him throughout his incarceration, and he could not believe his luck that someone as lovely as her, even though she was always heavily made-up, should have taken to him the way she had.

He saw her come in through the door and walk towards him, her slim figure full of potential future pleasure. As she approached, he said, 'Hi, I wish you'd come every week instead of just once a month, but it's still good to see you.'

'I live a long way away and I work, so I can't come very often, but, you know, you excite me. I won't stop coming to see you.'

'What do you want to talk about?' said Simms.

'I want you to thrill me with stories of evil-doings.'

'You sure? I don't want to put you off.'

'You won't.'

Simms decided to test her and went on to tell her in detail about a rape that he and Barton had committed, knowing that the rape had been reported to the police at the time. McKesson had been convicted of it and both himself and Barton had got away with it and could not be tried again. They said that they had been on holiday in Spain in Tommy Babcock's villa at the time, Babcock had backed them up and McKesson swore that they were not with him.

This was calculated, to test her loyalty to him. Should the police attend the prison to question him about it, he would know for sure that she was part of a set-up.

Chapter Sixteen

Delany got a call from Sergeant Thompson asking him to go to the local police station. On arrival, Thompson said, 'It's as you said; a week ago, we got a call about a minor bump at one of the roundabouts you pointed out and low and behold it was a front end shunt and the other driver had left the scene, I went and asked for traffic to attend.'

'Who was the driver?'

'A man called James Ringway, with his wife Sophia in the passenger seat; when we got there, he was protesting, saying he did not want the police to attend but was reporting it because he thought he had to.'

'Were they claiming any injury?'

'His wife said her neck was hurting a bit, but that's all, Ringway got quite uppity when I said that we were taking paint samples from his car to see if we could get a match with an offending vehicle. He kept saying that we had no right to be involved as it was only a minor bump.'

'Anything from Bennett's Land Rover?'

'Yea, just coming to that, I got a warrant on the strength of what you told me and went to Bennett's place, the tow bar had a recent paint smear, the same colour as Ringway's car. I had that checked over with forensics and it matched.'

'So you've got him for a drive away.'

'A bit more than that, Josh, I know of your reputation for thoroughness, so I've had a team searching the local scrap yard for the other vehicles involved in the previous bumps, and believe it or not, we found three waiting to be scrapped, all of which could be connected to the Land Rover due to minute paint traces. Come on, give me a clap.'

'Well done, Frank, so what now?'

'Well, the investigation has gone to the fraud squad, it's ongoing and looks like, eventually, they will all be charged with fraud.'

Gerald Nesbitt was at work in his office. He had previously been a regular police officer, and when he had retired, he had been taken on as a civilian scenes of crime officer. It was four o'clock on a Friday afternoon, and he was looking forward to his weekend off when he was due to play in a local golf tournament. His mobile phone rang.

'Gerald, it's Tommy. I need to see you.'

Nesbitt took his phone out into the corridor.

'Tommy, you know I don't like you ringing me at work.'

'I know, but it's urgent. I need to see you, come to mine tomorrow morning at ten.'

'But, Tommy, I'm in a golf tournament tomorrow, starting in the morning.'

'Cancel. I want to see you in the morning.'

Nesbitt knew better from long and bitter experience than to argue over the phone with Tommy Babcock.

'OK. I'll see you at ten.'

The following morning, Nesbitt arrived at Babcock's house and was ushered straight in to the rear lounge.

'I've a job for you.'

'Tommy, I'm always glad to work for you, the money's very good, but you should get your people to keep me informed. That last flat you got me to clean up was a close-run thing. Nobody told me that there was a body outside below, in the stairwell. I was taking my time cleaning it with those two baboons of yours when the coppers found the body. I only just got out in time.'

'Yea, but this one's not risky, Gerald, you know I pay you well and, in any case, you owe me, it was me who got that cheating, thieving wife of yours off your back.'

'I know, I came to you for a favour, but as you know, I only wanted her frightened off, not raped and drowned by the ape of yours, Baron.'

'We'll come to Baron later, you know McKesson.'

'The guy who was shot dead in the street?'

'Yea, him. Well, what you don't know is that it was his information that set up the cops' raid and the arrest of one of my best men Ramsay Simms, he's gone now and I'm not mourning McKesson, he was always a bit of a loser, but I know that the information the cops got was by force. I am also doubtful about the death of Tony Baron. He was covered in bruises, but the inquest ruled that they came from the cage fight the night before. The cause of death was drowning, I'm not having it that he simply fell in and drowned, he was too fit for that and, in any case, you don't have to be a good swimmer, that canal is only about five feet deep. If he had been any other member of Joe Public, there would have been some kind of investigation, but Baron was well known to the cops and they would have been delighted with his death because they couldn't normally pin anything on him. I don't think for a minute that the ordinary cops had anything to do with his death, but I do think that it must have been some kind of covert operation by undercover cops. What I want you to do is find out from your sources what the hell is going on and who is involved, before they get any closer to me.'

'OK, but I want payment, or I'm doing no more for you.'

'You'll do what I want you to do and whenever I want it. I've got enough black of you to send you away for many years; in any case, don't worry, you'll get paid.'

'I used to be pals with a leading light in under cover, I'll find out what I can.'

Simms was now in the penultimate month of his incarceration, seated in the visiting room, waiting for his Silvia; as she entered the room, he was delighted. He had tested her on her previous visit and was certain that she was genuine and not a police stooge.

'Great to see you. Not long to go now, things have been going wrong on the outside; with me in here, they can't cope, two of my old mates are dead; when I get out, the boss tells me I'll be his lead man, can't wait. I'll show you off to the boys then.'

'Go on, Ramsay, tell me another of your stories, you really thrilled me last time with your juicy tales of rape. You must have many more tales to tell me.'

'Well, there is one, a silly bint from the university and her boyfriend thought they could set us up with the cops and get away with it; they got a hell of a shock when me, Eddie and Tony walked in.'

'What happened then?'

'Well, she was a bonny lass, not as bonny as you mind, but bonny enough. We had been told to frighten off herself and her boyfriend, but we are red-blooded men, you know what I mean, so we had our way with her before we saw her off.'

'How did you see her off?'

'Well, the canal's always the favourite, they get rid of the evidence.'

'What about her boyfriend?'

'He was easy, a bit of a wimp, Tony was a big lad, and the boyfriend was pushed in by one of the Johnsons. Tony waltzed him in and made him look at his girlfriend and the state she was in, she was being seen to by me at the time. The stupid sod tried to fight Baron, but he had no chance. Baron just whacked him a few times, then walked him straight through the room and out over the balcony on the other side, which happened to be about forty feet from the ground.'

Simms laughed aloud at the thought of this and said. 'You're not laughing, I thought that you would enjoy that.'

'I did, I loved it. What was she called, can you remember?'

'Yea, her name was in the Manchester paper that week. Holly something or other, I can't properly remember.'

'Listen, Ramsay, I'm busy at work and I can't come again till you get out. If it's OK with you, I've booked us into a holiday cottage in the Dales for a week, you can show me some of your rape techniques there,' she giggled, 'I'll have a taxi waiting outside on your release.'

'Wow, great. I'm sure Tommy will let me off for a week, that will really give me something to look forward to.'

'Sorry, Tommy who?'

'Tommy Babcock, he's my boss.'

Chapter Seventeen

Silvia arrived at her flat in the Manchester Northern Quarter. As she walked through the door and into her empty apartment, she let out a huge scream of anguish and ran into her bedroom, wailing and crying bitterly, shouting at the top of her voice, 'The bastard, the bastard.' Her crying quietened down to a sobbing, and as she collapsed on her bed, the sobbing went on for over an hour before she could regain any kind of composure.

Eventually, she looked at herself in the mirror, taking off the blonde wig and washing away her tears and the heavy makeup, threw off the cheap tight clothing to regain her identity as Beverley Delany.

Nesbitt rang his old partner Jerry Saunders, 'Jerry, it's time we had a couple of pints together. What about this evening in the Bridgewater? It must be four or five years since we met up for a chat.'

'Sure, it will be good to see you, Gerald, I'll be in there tonight, about six, see you then.'

They met up at six for what Saunders thought was a convivial hour; after about forty minutes, Nesbitt said, 'Anything new you can tell me about?'

'I can't talk about my work, you know that, but I'll tell you who I met up with recently. Do you remember Josh Delany, worked around Manchester undercover for a while a few years ago?'

'Yes, I remember him, a bloody good cop.'

'His daughter was murdered in Manchester a few months ago in the university flats.'

'I remember that in the papers. I didn't know it was Josh's daughter.'

Nesbitt later reported the conversation back to Babcock, who commented, 'It looks like we have found the enemy.'

Delany was at home when Baldy called.

'I've had an interesting telephone call.'

'Go on.'

'Many years ago, I had a cellmate in Strangeways, a chap we all called Crabby Johnson. Do you remember telling me about the two lads who McKesson called doorkeepers when Holly was raped and murdered by the gang of ratbags?'

Baldy saw that the question put that way had badly upset Delany, who turned away to hide the tears which had surfaced.

'Sorry, Josh, but I have to tell you this, and there is no other way than straight.'

'Go on.'

'Well, he wants to meet me, he would not say why over the phone other than it is connected with you. I've offered to meet him at seven o'clock tomorrow night in the Dog & Pheasant, I'll find out what it's about then.'

'OK, I'm coming with you, he does not know me.'

'Only if you go as the old man, you know I love that disguise.'

The following evening, the two old men walked into the Dog & Pheasant at six thirty and were enjoying a pint when a third old man with a fat gut and sour face walked in, and Baldy walked across to him and hailed him with, 'Hi, Crabby.,

'Don't ever call me that again Baldy, my name is Benjamin and you know it,' he growled.

'Sorry, Benjamin, I thought you wanted me do something for you.'

Crabby lightened and almost smiled, 'Yea, I'm sorry too, Baldy, I thought I had lived that name down. Let me buy you a pint.'

'OK, and one for my mate.'

'Who the hell is he?'

'Don't you remember him? He was in Strangeways when we were, maybe in a different block, he's OK. You can say what you like in front of him, he's practically deaf anyway and he's lost most of his marbles, he does not know whether it's Tuesday or breakfast time, he never speaks. I only bring him out for old times' sake and the fact that he loves a pint or two. Whatever you say won't go any farther because he won't remember; in any case, he's one of the brotherhood.'

Over the next hour, Delany took the cue and played his part excellently, slurping the beer while staring into space and saying nothing.

'OK, Benjamin,' Baldy said at last, putting great emphasis on the name, 'What do you want?'

'Have you heard of an ex-copper called Delany, Josh Delany?'

'That bastard, he put me away at least twice, why?'

Delany's eyes twitched slightly, but he corrected himself.

'You've probably never heard of Tommy Babcock, he's a big wheel in the city, he's an old mate, well, ex-employer of mine. I was his bodyguard in the old days. He's put a thirty grand contract on Delany's head. I don't know why, but he wants Delany dead, my two boys want that money. They've worked for Babcock before on and off, and they're looking to go up in the world. All I want from you is a bit of crack, where does he live, who does he live with and when is the best time to get him and whatever else you can come up with.'

'What's in it for me?'

'Come on, we're mates, aren't we?'

'Only if you let me call you Crabby.'

'It's a deal, call me when you get the info.'

'I'll ring you as soon as I've got it.'

Crabby left soon afterwards, and Delany said immediately, 'Is he for real? He's obviously not the sharpest knife in the box.'

'Maybe not, but believe me, he is definitely for real, you should be very concerned.'

'Oh believe me, I am, what worries me most is how has Babcock got on to me, I've been covering my tracks like blazes, all I can think of is a slip, deliberate or not, by someone I have trusted.'

'I hope you're not looking at me.'

'No, 'course not, I've just had a great thought, do you remember I told you about the practicably derelict farmhouse that Hugh Bennett, the guy who got three years for fraud, lived in before he was sent down? We need to check it out, that's if you're still with me in this, bearing in mind we'll be up against some of your old mates.'

'With you all the way, whatever happens.'

The following day, Delany and Baldy checked out the old farm, it was well outside Lancaster, in the countryside and about half a mile off the main road, along its own farm track, the old farmhouse was locked up. Banging on the doors and peering through the windows, they could see clearly that whilst Bennett was inside prison, there were no current residents. The farm was situated in the cleft of a hill. There were no close neighbours. The farmhouse itself was of no interest to them, but examination of the large deserted barn and the equally abandoned stables proved that the place was perfect for the purpose.

'OK,' Delany said, 'This is perfect, ring old Crabby face and tell him this is where I live and that I always leave a light on in the old barn when I'm at home; see if you can get an idea of when they will come so we can be ready.'

'We?' Baldy said.

'Yep, you said all the way; anyway, this is payment for calling me a bastard.'

A few days later, Baldy rang Johnson.

'Benjamin, it's taken me a while to find out where Delany lives. He's in an old rundown farm off the main A 65, near Kirkby Lonsdale; it looks like he's doing it up. I've been sussing it out for you, and I can tell you that the barn light is always on when he is in, first thing he does when he gets there; he nearly had me one day when I was hiding out at the back of the barn and he came in. I had to sneak off across the fields to get away.'

He gave Crabby the post code for the house and said, 'Listen, I need to know exactly when your boys are coming down here; the local cops know that I hate Delany for what he's done to me, and I will be first suspect on their list if anything happens to him. I'll need a cast iron alibi when they come for me.'

'OK, I'll let you know.'

An hour later, Crabby rang back, 'Friday night, around midnight, sort your alibi out.'

Baldy reported back to Delany, 'Josh, Crabby's not exactly a mate of mine. But we have shared a cell and I don't want him to have to mourn his two lads, I've heard that they are a bit like their dad, not that bright. I don't know what Babcock is thinking about sending those two.'

'I am aware that they were around when Holly was raped and murdered, they were guarding the door, so they are not exactly innocent, but they did not rape or kill her themselves. Whatever they get on Friday night, they will deserve, but I'm not going to kill them, just make sure that they do not come back for more.'

'You do appreciate that they will be carrying guns and we won't, don't you?'

'Guns are only of use if you know how to use them efficiently, I'm making an assumption that they don't. Come on, let's get over there and start planning this thing, could be the sort of entertainment that I've been looking for.'

Chapter Eighteen

On the appointed evening, Delany and Baldy arrived at the farm early to set the scene for the arrival of the Johnson brothers. Delany had taken a car battery and managed to get the old Land Rover which was still parked in the barn running nicely.

He left the lights of the vehicle on and also rigged up a lamp from the battery, which he hung over one of the rafters.

Using the can of petrol he had brought, he started up the generator sited in a cabin at the rear of the house, and to his delight, three outside lights and an inside hall light came on without any further attention.

He and Baldy set their stall out around the barn and stables, then settled down in a quiet, dark corner, where they could see anything coming along the farm track, to await the arrival of their adversaries.

As he waited, he began to have doubts about the wisdom of their actions, hoping that the brothers were not particularly adept at subterfuge and silent movement; otherwise, he and Baldy were in grave danger. 'Are we about to be outsmarted?' he whispered to himself.

'What?' said Baldy.

'Nothing, mate,' he replied.

Just after midnight, his worst fears were dispelled as a loud roaring came from over the hill, and, suddenly, a car came into sight with full headlamps blazing and slurred to a stop just outside the farm gate.

'Ah,' said Delany, 'not a sneak attack then.'

The Johnson brothers got out of the car, which they left running with the lights on. It was a clear moonlit night, Delany could see them well enough as they climbed over the wide gate; they were both bulky lads, and from the way in which they climbed, he guessed that they were not particularly fit young men.

It seemed what they did not expect to find was mud, as they both appeared from the distance to be wearing trainers and the muddy drive took them by surprise as they plodded, and occasionally slipped, warily through it towards the barn where Delany and Baldy lurked. They each had a torch which they were shining on the drive and towards the barn haphazardly. Ominously, they were both carrying a revolver of some description.

Delany heard one of the brothers say, 'There's a light on and I can hear an engine running, he must be in.'

Delany and Baldy sneaked to the rear of the barn and Baldy slipped out of the back door and into the back door of the stable block.

Delany took a hammer from the bench and began to bang heavily on the bench.

Outside, the brothers heard the banging, and approaching the barn door, Flash said, 'This is going to be easy, charge the door, we both shoot him twice, then away, are you ready?' Sparkler shouted, 'Yea, let's go.'

They ran together, both kicking out at the door which gave way easily; as they ran in, they both saw two figures running towards them. They fired together two shots each. There was a loud crashing noise and the running figures disappeared. The brothers were temporarily stunned until Flash, who was the sharper of the two, realised that they had just destroyed a huge full-length mirror image of themselves.

As they ran in, Delany exited through the back door and into the rear yard, where he picked up a rope and delayed for a second or two whilst the brothers re-orientated themselves.

Flash looked quickly around the barn and saw a figure standing on a bench beside an open window. He fired four shots at the figure.

Delany then pulled the rope and the scarecrow-type dummy he had constructed earlier came flying through the window, across a slope and into the yard.

It seemed to Flash that the figure dived through the window into the yard behind. He shouted to Sparkler, 'He's jumped through that window, go 'round the back, he has to be wounded, and we'll get him there.'

Sparkler ran out from where they came in and ran into the stable block. To get to the back yard, he assumed he would have to go through the stable.

Flash ran across to the window, climbed onto the bench and saw the figure standing by the house wall about ten yards away; he pulled the trigger, but this time, the gun was empty. He ducked down behind the window and quickly reloaded.

As he looked up again, the figure was still there; as he fired, the figure appeared to duck down on to the ground. He shouted, 'Sparkler, are you there?' There was no reply. He shouted, 'Shit, I have to do everything.'

The ground outside the window appeared to be a solid grassy slope down the yard, and he reasoned that that was how Delany had escaped.

He jumped from the bench, on to the window sill and out on to the slope.

The slope was not what it appeared to be in the moonlight. It was, in fact, a six feet deep pile of cow and horse muck which had been lying there for many years. So long, that it had acquired over the years a layer of grass and a six-inch crust which immediately gave way under the considerable weight of Flash Johnson. He plunged into the muck well over his head. The gun and the torch were lost from his grip as he struggled to get to his feet and out of his well-planned predicament.

Sparkler, in the meanwhile, searched for a way to the rear of the barn, it came to him that the quickest way was via the stables. The stable door was ajar. In his hurry, he shoulder-charged the door and entered.

Baldy was hidden in one of the stable units under a pile of straw, he estimated where in the stables Sparkler was from the sound of his footsteps, and when he was in the centre of the block, Baldy pulled the first of his two ropes. As he did, an eight gallon tank of old tractor engine oil, which had been painstakingly set in the rafters earlier that day by Baldy and Delany, upturned and crashed down on him, covering him from head to toe in black filth.

Sparkler fell to the ground, trying desperately to wipe the stinging oil from his eyes, his gun and torch slipping from his hands and being long-forgotten.

Flash eventually extricated himself from the muck after falling headlong into it on a couple of occasions and having the similar problem of wiping the filth from his eyes so that he could see dimly. He staggered through the rear door of the stables, where he saw Sparkler who was obviously in more distress than he was himself.

As he reached Sparkler, he shouted, 'Let's get the hell out of here.' Baldy pulled the second rope of his own little booby trap, which released several pounds of fine white feathers from the netting they had placed above.

The brothers, by this time, were shaking and delirious, looking like two large Christmas snowmen, they staggered and slipped out of the stables, then ran as quickly as they could, sliding and falling in the mud a couple of times, back to the awaiting car, which roared away back towards the main road and away from their humiliation as quickly as they possibly could.

Baldy and Delany were in hysterics with laughter.

Eventually, when he could speak, Delany said, 'I'm glad now that you kept that old feather mattress; I'll tell you what, I can't believe that Babcock sent those two idiots to do his business.'

Baldy replied, wiping tears from his eyes, 'He is obviously losing respect in the city due to the loss of his top men and the raid on his drug empire and can't find anyone else to do his bidding. I don't think you will be troubled by those two again.'

'Why are they called Flash and Sparkler'?

'Flash has convictions for flashing, exposing himself to girls in Heaton Park, and Sparkler has a major fetish for fireworks.'

They set about retrieving the guns to destroy them. Delany lost the toss and was forced to delve in the dung heap.

In fact, the two brothers were never seen in Manchester again. No one, even their father, had any idea what had happened to them, it was assumed in some quarters they had been assassinated by Babcock or one of his rivals in the drug trade, but nobody knew the truth, except, of course, the brothers themselves, assuming they were still alive.

Baldy's theory was that they were so humiliated at the barn that they decided to change their identities and live elsewhere. In fact, he hoped that they had changed their lives completely and were reasonably content as, unlike their father, they never had been the material of serious villains.

Babcock's empire was crashing in upon him, the loss of Barton and the drug raid had made great inroads into his drug business. Others in the city had seen the opportunity and had moved in on his empire. His frustration was all consuming. He misconstrued the disappearance of the brothers assuming they had failed in their mission and been totally eliminated.

His general lack of fitness and his previous indolent lifestyle was also catching up with him, so much so that on awakening one morning, he felt a crushing pain in his chest and along his left arm. He lay in bed, gasping for breath, and his wife called for the ambulance.

Baldy called on Delany, 'I've got some good news for you. I've just heard on the grapevine that Babcock has had a massive heart attack and is in intensive care.'

'Oh no, that's not good news as far as I am concerned. I need him to tell me who was the flat cleaner after Holly's murder. I think he or she is connected with the police. Whoever it is, they will have to pay the price, and I can't think of any other way of getting that information except through Babcock. Will you keep an eye on his progress for me?'

With Babcock laid up in hospital and Simms still serving his prison sentence, Delany was able to spend more time with his work for Pasternac Solicitors. Most of it was routine.

The insurers for the local authority had received dozens of claims from residents who said they had tripped and fallen over uneven pavements after dark on the High Street, causing injury to themselves. Pasternacs were asked to investigate. Delany attended the relevant stretch of road, he checked and, sure enough, the pavements were in a mess, broken and uneven, probably due to cars parking upon them. He mused to himself, *Surely the problem is solved by simply fixing the pavements.*

He spotted a café across the road from the offending pavements and decided that he would return at dusk and have his evening meal and coffee there, at lease he thought, *I will have paid some attention to the problem, but my report will simply recommend repairing the uneven pathway.*

Just after it became dark, Delany returned to the café, asked for a window seat and ordered his evening meal, which turned out to be rather good. Nothing happened across the road, and Delany did not really expect anything else. However, the meal was so good that he decided to linger with a large glass of good quality red wine.

As he sipped, a car pulled up across the way and two men got out, they opened the rear door and pulled a middle-aged lady from the rear seat, she was limping badly and could hardly walk, even from the distance Delany could see that her legs were bruised and bleeding and that she had some kind of nasty recent injury, he started his camera rolling.

The two men then gently laid her on the pavement where it was at its worst. One man got into the car and drove away. The other man made a telephone call.

Delany could clearly see what was happening and was shaking with laughter at the table, drinking his wine. So much so, that a waitress came to him and said, 'Can I help you, sir?'

He said, 'I've just seen a drama across the road where a woman, who has obviously been injured somewhere else, is pretending she has fallen over the pavement.'

'Oh, they are always doing that there. I don't know why they don't mend the bloody flags,' she replied.

A short time later, an ambulance came and took the lady and her escort away.

Delany put in his report with the rider that the only long-term solution was repair. He did, however, decide that he would not hold his breath until the repair was carried out.

He later found out that the lady in question had fallen in her own garden and had been persuaded by her two sons to fake the accident elsewhere for the compensation money.

Chapter Nineteen

Beverley, alias Silvia, paid her final prison visit to Simms. 'Where have you been, I've not seen you for months, I thought you'd given up on me. Anyway, I'm glad you've come, they're letting me out at long last. I've got my release date; the 20th of next month, I thought we could get it together.'

'The 20th of January, I didn't think you'd be out for ages. I thought you got three years.'

'Yea, I'm coming out on licence. I've heard Babcock's in hospital, so I'll be after a new employer,' he said with a snigger, 'But first, you and I should get to know each other better, if you know what I mean.'

Beverley had to think quickly, 'Oh, I know exactly what you mean, and I want the same thing, too. I'll be waiting outside with the taxi when you get out. My parents have a holiday cottage up north of here, we'll go up there for a few days if you want.'

'Bring it on. Bring it on.'

'OK, leave the arrangements to me,' she said.

She rang Delany that evening and told him what had transpired. He was unaware that she had been visiting Simms and was shaken by what she said.

'OK,' he said, 'leave the taxi to me. I don't want you further involved, you've done more than enough already.' Beverley argued that she was in this just as deeply as he was, but Delany was adamant that she should take no further part in what was to happen next.

'By the way, he does not know you as Beverley, does he?'

'Of course not, dad, do you think I'm a complete amateur? He thinks I'm called Silvia.'

'OK, Silvia, your work's done.'

The following morning, Delany scoured the for-sale advertisements for a suitable elderly vehicle which could become a convincing taxi. He found one, an old black cab which he bought using a false name and address and with no intention of registering it in his name, he took it to the old farmhouse for conversion.

At nine forty-five in the morning of the 20th of January, a black cab pulled up outside HM Prison Strangeways, the driver waited patiently, watching the door intently.

Prisoners, on release, began to leave the prison one by one until the driver spotted the man he was looking for. He got out of the cab, walked towards the man and said, 'Mr Simms?'

'Who's asking?'

'I've been asked to pick you up by Silvia and take you to her place up near Lancaster.'

'I thought she would be here herself.'

'No, she said she couldn't make it personally, but I know where to take you to, jump in.'

Simms walked towards the front passenger seat, the old man said, 'No, in the back please, I'm not licensed to carry passengers in the front.'

The old man opened the rear door on the nearside and Simms began to get in, looking along the road as he did so. He got back off the seat and said, 'I thought you said she wasn't coming, here she is.'

The old man looked up and saw a brassy blonde woman approaching. 'Hi,' she said, approaching Simms, 'I got free of my appointments and decided to meet you here after all.' Simms did not see the look of fury on the old man's face.

He got back out of the car, ran up to the woman and held her in an embrace, with his hand clutching her bottom and pulling her heavily towards himself and, at the same time, leering towards other ex-prisoners as they came out of the prison door, yelling, 'Bet you haven't got one like this to come out to.'

The old man could see the grimace that the blonde had on her face, attempting to make it look like a smile.

Eventually, Simms and Silvia came to the cab. The old man said to Simms, 'In the back please.' Simms returned through the nearside door and sat, waiting for Silvia. 'Seat belt please,' said the old man.

'Nah, I never wear seat belts,' came the reply.

'In which case, we are going nowhere,' the old man shouted stubbornly.

'Put your damn seat belt on,' shouted Silvia, 'I've paid for this cab, and it's cost me a fortune.' Simms reluctantly clicked his seat belt into place.

'Thank you, now you', he said pointing at Silvia, 'get in the front seat.' I'm not having any fornication in my cab, it's too precious to me.'

What, this old thing precious? You've got to be joking, it's a bloody old relic like you, you daft old bugger. Anyway, you said I couldn't sit in the front.'

'Well, she's a bit prettier than you.'

'Ramsay, let it be,' said Silvia. 'It's only an hour or so of a ride, then we can do what we want,' she said, looking directly at the old man.

They set off through the city and on to the M 62 motorway with Simms, clearly intending to irritate the old man making obscene remarks constantly to Silvia about what he was going to do to her once they were alone.

'We'll have no salacious talk on the journey, thank you very much,' said the old man, pressing a switch which sent the transparent dividing-screen sliding quietly upwards, cutting off all hearing and conversation between the compartments.

'You shouldn't be here. You know what I have to do to this bastard, and I don't want you involved.'

'Dad, I hate this guy as much if not more than you do, having had to suffer his company and his bragging about killing my sister and getting away with it. I'm in this all the way, and there is nothing you can do to stop me.'

'Yes, there is; I could stop and eject you from this car.'

'And then what trouble you will have with the idiot back there. Look, I don't know exactly what you are planning to do, but I've a fair idea and know it won't be pleasant, but I would like to give him one last chance of admitting his guilt before we do anything else. Then if he won't, it's back to your plan A.'

'OK, you're on.'

They reached the M6, and as they drove north, Simms decided that wearing the seat belt did not suit his macho style. And as much to irritate the cab driver as for any other reason, he felt for the release button and found that it was missing; he wriggled his fingers about inside the switch, to no avail. He could not unfasten the seat belt.

Simms reached forward as far as he could and banged on the screen; Silvia turned towards him, smiled sweetly, then turned away, the driver did not respond at all.

Simms struggled with the safety belt, but all he succeeded in doing was to tighten it even more, so much so that he could no longer reach the screen to bang on it. He began to shout and scream at the top of his voice, but the two in the front seats either could not hear him or simply ignored the shouting.

The old man driving the cab said, 'This is the very reason I did not want you to take any part in this, we are going to have to stay in disguise if we are to try to reason with this idiot, we'll try to find somewhere quiet.'

The cab left the motorway and set off up into the moorland of the West Pennines. From his position in the rear seat, Simms could see that the old man and Silvia were having a conversation and ignoring his predicament with the seat belt; as time went on, it began to dawn upon him that he was a prisoner once more and that something was seriously afoot. He struggled more and more with the seat belt, shouting and screaming in such a way that they must surely hear him, but there was no response from either of them. By this time, he was becoming seriously frightened.

The cab was driven down a long steep hill; as it approached a bridge and sharp left-hand bend at the bottom of the hill, the old man was driving a little too quickly in his hurry to get this over with.

A sheep ran suddenly from the left in front of the speeding vehicle. The old man braked sharply and skidded to the right, bouncing from the stonework of the bridge and spinning in the road, before it came to a stop.

The old man and Silvia were briefly stunned by the impact and sat dazedly in their seats.

The crash did what Simms had failed to do and snapped the mechanism of the previously-tampered-with-locked seat belt, freeing Simms, who shot forward and collided with the cab screen.

Simms was the first to recover and quickly saw his opportunity; he got out of the cab, looked around and saw a thick branch of wood lying in the grass at the side of the road.

The old man began to recover and shouted to his daughter, 'Are you all right?'

'Yes,' she shouted in return.

He turned and saw that Simms had escaped, he opened the driver's door and started to get out of the cab, he was halfway out when Simms struck him heavily over the head with the branch. The old man collapsed to the ground, semi-conscious.

Simms then threw the branch to the ground and ran off uphill, back the way they had driven. Silvia ran to the old man, who shouted, 'I'm OK, just dazed, get after him, and I'll follow best I can.'

She ripped the blonde wig from her head and threw it onto the grass verge in disgust and set off up the hill after Simms. She was now the vengeful Beverley in pursuit of the man she hated.

By now, Simms had a several-hundred-yard start on her, he was reasonably fit and very muscular and strong after his spell in prison where he had been well fed and had exercised with weights, but he was no runner. Beverley, however, was supremely fit and a regular runner, she began to quickly overhaul Simms.

They had been running for about half a mile when Simms looked over his shoulder and saw that she was only about a hundred yards behind him and there was no one else in sight, he was badly out of breath by now and gasped to himself, 'Why am I running away from a girl?'

He saw a copse just ahead; when he got there, he turned left off the road and ran along a track through the bushes; fifty yards along the track, he ducked behind a laurel hedge and waited.

As Beverley approached the hedge, he leapt out from his hiding place and confronted her.

He saw that she was sweating which had smudged her heavy makeup, she now had dark flowing hair and looked incredibly beautiful in a rugged way.

Simms now knew he had the advantage, she was fitter than him, but he was, by far, the stronger of the two.

She tried to confuse him by saying, 'Come back to the cab, we can carry on where we left off.'

'No chance. I don't know who you are, but you're not the Silvia who saw me in the prison; anyway, I can get all I want here.'

'He stepped forward and struck her hard in the face with his fist, she reeled backwards and fell into the hedge, Simms kicked her in the side and shouted, 'Now you do what I want; that old guy is out of it, he can't help you,' he kicked her again and fell on top of her, holding her arms down and head-butted her in the face.

By this time, Beverley was dazed and hurt, her resistance was declining, but she was able to shout and scream at him, 'Get off me, you bastard.'

'Who the hell are you, you crazy bitch?' he yelled.

She yelled, 'I'm Holly's sister, the girl you raped and murdered in Manchester.'

'Ah,' he shouted delightedly, 'Now I'm going to rape and murder you, you stupid bitch.'

Beverley began to regain her strength and pushed back at him, screaming with all her might as he tried to tug at her jeans.

He hit her again with his fist, and she screamed again. He grabbed her throat with his left hand and began to rip at her jeans, attempting to pull them down with his right.

The old man lay on his back for a few moments after being struck. His eyes were out of focus and he was seeing double and the world swam in front of him.

He slowly came back to his senses, shook his head vigorously, his thinking returned and he became Delany again.

He jumped to his feet suddenly, fully aware of the predicament his daughter was in. He shouted in anguish, 'If anything had happened to her, I'll never forgive myself.' He picked up the branch which had floored him and took off up the hill.

He was unable to see either his daughter or Simms as he ran along, and as he got to the top of the hill, he heard a scream from the woods to his left, he ran that way and heard a second scream a few yard ahead. He suddenly saw the back of Simms obviously struggling with Beverley, although he could not see her.

Delany smashed the wood hard on Simms' head, he collapsed under the impact.

Beverley, who was starting to feel herself slipping into unconsciousness, felt Simms suddenly loosen his grip on her and fall on top of her, she gasped for breath and pushed as hard as she was able to and he fell away to one side. She saw her father staring down at her and began to sob. She shouted in distress, 'Dad, look away please, tugging at her jeans and pulling them up.'

Delany looked away, appalled. She got to her feet, and they stood for several minutes, hugging each other.

Eventually, she said, 'Don't worry, Dad, he did not have time to do anything to me.'

'Thank God for that,' said Delany.

Even though Simms was heavily unconscious, Delany tied his hand and feet with his own boot laces.

Beverley went down the hill for the cab, which she found still drivable, even though it was badly damaged. They dragged Simms back to the road and threw him into the capacious luggage space at the rear, locking it tight.

Delany drove again, and they headed straight for Nibs Quarry. On arrival, Delany opened a farm gate and said to Beverley, 'You know where my car is parked, go and sit in it, and I'll be with you in about half an hour or so.'

This time she did as she was asked to do and walked away down the lane. Delany drove the cab through the meadow, along a farm track and to a disused field which sloped gently down to a sheer drop of about thirty feet into the flooded quarry. He parked the cab a few feet from the drop and facing the quarry.

With a great effort, he dragged the still unconscious Simms from the rear luggage space and sat him in the driver's seat with the engine still running, he clicked the seat belt into place, retrieved his boot laces, opened all the windows, then entered the cab from the passenger side and placed a weight with a rope attached on the clutch, holding it down. He placed Simms' right foot on the accelerator and pushed the driver's seat uptight to stop it from slipping off. He put the cab in first gear, released the handbrake and got slowly and quietly out of the cab, then anchored the rope to a stake in the ground and slowly pulled the weight off the clutch.

The cab moved forward slowly to the quarry's brim, and the weight was dragged out from the still-open passenger door. The cab toppled quietly over the edge, completely turning over, and fell into the water roof first, and with all the windows and passenger door open, it sank like a brick into the fifty-feet depth.

He stood looking down at the water for about ten minutes to ensure the success of his mission.

Delany threw the weight and rope into a different part of the quarry and then walked back through the fields and along the lane to where his car was parked with Beverley inside.

'Is it over?'

'Yes, you know I never wanted you to be involved in any of this.'

'I know, but it's all over now, isn't it?'

'Yes,' lied Delany, knowing full well that it was not yet over, but not wanting Beverley to take any further part.

Chapter Twenty

Tommy Babcock was asleep in the intensive care unit when the doctor came doing his rounds. He spoke to the nurse, 'Can you wake him gently, I want to have a chat with him and put him in the picture?'

She stroked Babcock's face until he awoke. The doctor spoke, 'Good afternoon, Mr Babcock, sorry to wake you up. We have done all our tests. I don't want to upset you too much, but I can now tell you that you have had quite a large heart attack, but with the medication you are on, and will be on in the future, there is no reason for us to think that you cannot live to a good old age, provided that you take your medication and retire from any stressful employment. I understand that you are sixty-five years of age. You should now live a quiet sedentary life, away from the hurly-burly, take a little exercise at first, say, just strolling around your garden and build up gradually to maybe gentle swimming or short country walks.'

'Will I ever be able to return to my normal work?'

'Well, I don't know what that was, but I cannot recommend it.'

'What about an operation to put me right?'

'Due to your age and general condition, I do not think that is practicable at this time. However, I cannot rule anything out in the future. Goodness, who knows what the future holds for any of us, we will keep you here for another couple of days, then you will be fit enough to return home. But please bear in mind what I have said.'

Babcock indeed returned home two days later, where he mulled over his future, he was well aware that his empire in

Manchester was over, he had lost his main men and, in any case, other people had quickly moved in during his absence. He was also aware that was at least partially due to the interference in his affairs by a certain Josh Delany. He rang his old employee, Crabby.

'Did your boys see to things up north while I was stuck in hospital?'

'Sorry, boss I've not heard from them; in fact, none of their mates have seen them since before they went up there, I'm really worried that things have gone wrong, I'll find out and get back to you.'

'Listen, Crabby, I want to see you here, I've got another proposition to make to you as an old mate and comrade at arms. I think this one will be right up your street, let me know about your boys, I would like to hear that their business venture was successful.'

He spoke to his wife, 'We have enough money set aside for our retirement and we have our villa in Spain.'

They began to plan their future lives in the sunshine, as they had always intended.

He spoke to Gerard Nesbitt, the ex-police officer and current scenes of crime officer who had cleaned Holly's flat following the rape and murder. 'Gerry, I'm retiring, just thought I'd let you know.'

'I'll miss you, Tommy, but I'll miss your money more, no offence.'

'Are you interested in working for Frankie Maxwell?'

'Yea, if he pays as well as you do.'

'Leave it to me, I'll arrange it.'

Tommy rang Frankie Maxwell, the younger man who had usurped him and had taken over the illegal drug trade in the city.

'Frankie. It's Tommy Babcock, it's time we had a chat.'

Maxwell was highly suspicious; in the recent past, Babcock had made several attempts on his life.

'What the hell do you want, Babcock? You need to know that I'm the boss now and I'm giving nothing away.'

'Frankie, Frankie, Frankie, it's time we were friends. I know we've had our differences, shall we say, but I'm no longer in the market. I'm retiring, you don't need to know the reason why, but I'm going to put my feet up abroad. I'm ringing because I've got something to sell to you, something that will be very beneficial to you, where and when can we meet?'

'Come on, is this another of your little games? I'm not for sale in any way.'

'I appreciate that; listen, let's meet for a small drink, you can bring a couple of your boys if you want, there are no tricks. I'm just trying to make a few extra pennies before I retire, and you will want what I have got for sale.'

'Give me a clue of what you're selling.'

'Not over the phone, you know how things are as well as I do.'

'Whatever it is, what's the price?'

'It's ten grand cash, bring it with you, it will be worth every penny, believe me.'

On the evening before the meeting, Crabby attended at Babcock's house as arranged.'

'I've managed to get hold of Gerald at long last.'

'Who's Gerald?'

'Oh sorry, you know him as Flash, one of my sons, something went very wrong up north, they didn't get Delany. I don't know why, he wouldn't tell me. Him and Harry, my other son, ended up in a hospital somewhere. Anyway, they are not coming back to Manchester, they won't tell me why or where they are, just that I am not likely to see them again. To be honest, they are no bloody loss, they always were a bit pathetic, I blame their wimp of a mother.'

'Listen, Ben, I've got something that will cheer you up. I'm going to move out to my place in Spain, you know the one, you've been there before.'

'Yea, the one with the high walled garden.'

That's the one, I want you to come with me, you know there is a high gate and small apartment just inside the gate, that's yours if you want it. You can be my eyes and ears, nobody will come in or go out without your say so, what do you think?'

'When do we go?'

'Listen, I'm going to meet Frankie Maxwell shortly, I want you to come with me.'

'I'm no match for Frankie's boys nowadays.'

'You don't need to be. There won't be any problems, I just want you to sit in a corner and look menacing.'

They chose a city centre public house for the meeting and a time of two in the afternoon as both parties were suspicious of each other and expected some kind of trap.

Babcock arrived first and sat in a conspicuous position in the centre of the lounge, leaving a seat for one person opposite. Crabby sat at the far end of the bar, scowling and looking as menacing as he possibly could, given his advancing age.

Maxwell entered with a swagger, followed by two large glowering gentlemen who sat at the bar on either side of Crabby, who they had recognised, both giving him evil looks from both sides.

Crabby was no longer sure who to scowl at and tried it on both sides alternatively, then gave up and stared into his pint.

'Afternoon, Frankie, good of you to come, you really didn't need your bodyguards.'

'No, but I notice you've brought yours.'

'Who, Crabby? He's too old to be dangerous.'

'Come to the point, Tommy, what have you got to sell that I would be remotely interested in?'

'OK, lean closer. When you or your boys attend a, shall we say, incident, does it ever cross your mind that you may have overlooked something about which the cops can later point the finger at you, anything at all, however small and insignificant it may seem to you at the time?'

'Yea, 'course I do, that's how sometimes even the most careful of us end up in the slammer.'

'Well, I have the very tonic for the malady. The name and number of an ex-cop and current scenes of crime chap who's no longer any use to me, he'll work for you if you pay him well enough and clean up any mess you or any of your boys make. Are you interested?'

'So you really are retiring then and trying to make a few bob wherever you can. If I pay you, how do I know he will work for me?'

'I tell you he is only interested in money; if you have any problems with him, let me know, I have enough on him to put him away for the rest of his born natural.'

The deal was made, and Gerald Nesbitt was sold to Frankie Maxwell.

While this was going on, Crabby and the Maxwell boys had decided to lose their enmity and were happily drinking together and swapping tall stories.

Chapter Twenty-One

Delany and Baldy were talking. Delany said, 'I wonder how Babcock is doing, we haven't heard from him for a while. Do you think you could get some information from Crabby if you rang him?'

'I can try, but he might be a bit suspicious of me after what happened to his boys.'

Baldy rang and Crabby answered, 'Hi, mate, it's Baldy, how you doing?'

'Baldy, it's good to hear from you.'

Baldy smiled and nodded to Delany.

'I thought I'd just check how your lads are. I've seen that bastard Delany around, so I know they didn't get him.'

'They're bloody useless those two. Something went wrong, I don't know what. They've been in touch and they're staying away from Manchester, they don't seem to want to know me anymore. I've no idea where they are or what went wrong, bloody good riddance I say.'

'How's your old boss Babcock? I've heard he was in hospital.'

'Yea, he had a nasty heart attack and he's finishing work, if you know what I mean, and retiring to Spain. He's got a place just outside Lloret de Mar on the Costa Blanca, and believe it or not, I'm going with him as his gate-keeper-cum-bodyguard.'

'Bodyguard, pull the other one, Crabby, you're much too old for that.'

'Eh, you're no spring chicken yourself.'

The conversation went on for a while. When he rang off, Delany remarked to Baldy, 'Looks like we might get a nice holiday out of this.'

For the Babcock family, things went ahead smoothly; they sold their detached house in Altrincham on the outskirts of Manchester for an excellent price. The shipment of some furniture to Spain and the sale of furniture and other fittings also went well and they were ready to move out permanently to Lloret de Mar.

Crabby did not have much to sell, his wife had left him years before and his boys were no longer in touch. He left Manchester happily.

Babcock had owned the villa for some years, and it had always been his intention to move there upon retirement.

When they arrived at the villa, even though he had been there before, Crabby could not believe his good luck; it was stunning. A large four-bed villa set in its own grounds, with a ten-foot high wall all the way around and a small one-bed flat adjacent to the double gates which were the only entrance and exit from the property.

Maid, gardening and chauffeur service was easily arranged from the local town of Lloret de Mar.

Crabby was given his orders by Babcock, 'The gate house is your private place, nobody comes or goes without your say so. You'll soon get to know the servants, you can wave them through. Anybody else turns up, you come and speak to me; they only come in on my say so. You'll get all your meals laid on and your flat cleaned, but you must be vigilant at all times; otherwise, you're back to Manchester and I'll find someone else. Understand?'

'Yea, boss, no problem, just happy to be here.'

'Come on then, Crabby, let's have a drink and celebrate being here.'

Baldy called upon Delany, 'When are we going on holiday to Spain? I am really looking forward to it.'

'Let's give them a few months to settle in and feel secure and confident, then we'll go and spoil their little comfortable dream, do we know where the villa is?'

'No, shall I try to find out?'

'No, that would just make them suspicious, we'll find them when we get there.'

Two months later, Delany and Baldy set off on a "holiday" to Lloret de Mar. They booked in at the Copacabana Hotel and began to enjoy the sunny surroundings of the Spanish seaside resort.

There were several European-owned bars in the town. When they had become established as regular customers, they began to tell people that they were interested in buying a place in the area and asked about any British newcomers to the area who may be able to give advice on where to buy and local prices.

In one bar, they were told that an English man called Ben had moved into the area recently and drank there occasionally and had a place on the edge of town, called Villa Toanba.

At first, this meant nothing to them and they set off towards the next bar, when suddenly Baldy said, 'Wait a minute. Eureka! We've found it.'

'What?'

'Toanba, Tommy and Ann Babcock. Ann's his wife's name, the first two letters of each name, Ben must be Crabby, get it, Benjamin Johnson? If I know Crabby, he will be pretending that the place is his.'

'Let's go take a look,' said Delany.

'You go on your own; if Crabby sees me with you, he will start to put two and two together.'

Delany soon found the place on the edge of town, heading out into the countryside. There was a bus stop opposite where he could sit and examine the building.

It was a detached building set in its own extensive grounds surrounded by a wall about ten feet high with what looked like glass spikes on top; from where he sat, he could just about see the roof above the wall. There was a high double gate and a much smaller villa inside the gate and what appeared to be a touch pad on the right of the gate. He also noted that he could not see any cameras facing the street.

A bus came along, so he strolled off for a few hundred yards, then came back and watched. It was by now four o'clock in the afternoon and he saw a young woman on the inside of the gate, she looked as though she was waiting to get out, and as he watched a man he recognised as Crabby appeared. Delany drew back behind the bus shelter and saw that Crabby also approached the gates from the inside and pressed what appeared to be a similar touch pad on the inside, the gates opened and the young woman walked out and set off towards the town.

Satisfied, Delany walked back into town and found Baldy in the bar where he had left him.

'You were spot on, Baldy. I didn't know you were good at cryptic clues; anyway, we now need a plan, and that's my department.'

Delany spoke to the barman who had mentioned the name Ben. 'It might be interesting to have a chat with Ben, he may be able to put me in the picture about buying around here. When is he likely to be in.'

'He sometimes strolls in at about one o'clock in the afternoon, has a couple of pints and is gone half an hour later.'

For the next two afternoons between noon and two, Baldy sat in the lounge bar, happily sipping pints of beer at Delany's expense, with no luck.

On the third attempt at exactly one o'clock, Crabby walked in and ordered a pint of beer, he sat at the bar and looked around the room. 'Bloody hell, Baldy, is that you?'

'My god, it's Crabby. What on earth brings you here?'

'I told you, don't call me Crabby. Anyway, you don't you remember that I said I was moving here to live.'

'I remember that you said Spain but I'd no idea where, I'm just here for a few days of sun and sangria. Well, fancy meeting you here, let's have a day on the pop together.'

'Can't, I'm working. Tommy just lets me out for a couple of pints every now and then.'

'We should meet up for old times' sake while I'm here.'

'Listen, he lets me have a couple of hours on a Saturday night late on, meet me here at eleven and we'll have a couple of hours in town.'

'I'll see you at your place.'

'No, no chance. Tommy would sack me if I let anybody in that he doesn't know, and I value my job too highly for that.'

Delany was again at the bus stop when Crabby returned from the bar, he watched as closely as he dared whilst Crabby put in the digits on the pad to open the gates. He clearly saw that Crabby made four distinct movements with his right hand, but was too far away and could not see for certain which numbers he pressed to get in. He noted, however, that Crabby pressed one high number on the pad, then one low number, then two more high numbers.

He looked around to ensure that he was not being watched, strolled across the road and, as unobtrusively as possible, took a close-up photograph of the key pad.

Back at the hotel, he studied the photograph on his camera and saw that four digits zero, one, two and nine were just very slightly duller in shade than the others.

Baldy walked into his room. 'Ah,' Delany said, 'They have not changed the numbers for a long time, laziness makes it slightly easier.'

He rang Beverley, 'Bev, Tommy Babcock was obviously well known to the police in Manchester, can you look up his date of birth for me?'

'Dad, I thought that was all finished and over with.'

'It is, well, almost, just clearing up a few matters.'

She rang back an hour later. 'Dad, it's the 29th of October, '38. I don't know why you want it, but do not put yourself in any more danger.'

'Thanks, love, don't worry, I'll be fine.'

He turned to Baldy, 'Spot on. 2910. It's what I thought.'

Chapter Twenty-Two

On Saturday evening, Delany and Baldy had one quiet drink together. It was a quiet, balmy evening. At ten thirty, Delany said, 'Keep him out as long as you can.' They split up, Baldy to the bar, where he was to meet Crabby, and Delany to the villa, where he slipped quietly into the shadows and waited.'

Just before eleven o'clock, Crabby walked out of the gates and away towards town.

Delany watched him until he was well out of sight. He approached the gates and pressed the four-digit number, he heard a distinctive click, pressed the gates, and they quietly opened. He slipped inside and moved off to his right, around the rear of the gate house, where he stopped in the darkness and looked towards the main villa.

He saw that there was a large French window facing a huge swimming pool. The window was open, and he could hear faint voices from inside.

Suddenly, a woman walked through the French window and an automatic light outside came on, illuminating the patio outside the windows and the swimming pool.

Now, Delany could see a camera above the window close to the light. He could not see any sign of an alarm, although he did not discount the possibility that there was one somewhere out of sight.

As she walked down the steps into the pool, he now heard her slightly slurred voice, 'I'm just doing a few lengths, then I'm off to bed.'

A male voice replied, 'I'll follow you in later.' That voice also sounded to Delany to be slurred.

The woman left the pool after six very slow lengths and walked back inside.

The light went out a few seconds later. Delany moved closer to the villa, out of range of the camera and the automatic light and waited in the dark.

He could now hear what was being said inside the still-open window. The woman's voice said, 'Right, I've taken my pill and I'm off to bed.'

The male voice said, 'Should you be taking those damn things after what you've had to drink?'

'I'm OK, I need my sleep, goodnight.'

Delany waited. Half an hour later, the man, who Delany easily recognised as Tommy Babcock, walked through the window and the light came on. Babcock threw his dressing gown to one side, and Delany noticed that he was completely naked. He got into the pool and began to swim very slow lengths.

Delany, wary of the camera, saw that a window at the side of the villa was open. He climbed through, ready at any time to abandon his plan if an alarm went off anywhere; none did.

Peeping through the window, he waited until Babcock was swimming away from the window, then he found where the camera wire came through the wall and into the house. He traced the wire to a socket and switched it off.

He walked to the foot of the staircase, where he could hear soft and gentle snoring from above.

He retraced his steps to the window and peeped through. Babcock was just starting a slow length away from the villa, Delany dropped his own clothes on the lounge floor and quietly walked across the patio and entered the water without a splash.

He swam slowly towards Babcock, waited until the other man was about to turn back in his direction, then dived deep and swam under Babcock, surfacing quietly behind him.

As he approached the centre of the pool, Delany said, 'Hello, Tommy.'

Babcock's immediate alarm was obvious, and without turning around, he began to swim as fast as he could towards the side of the pool. Delany, who was a considerably quicker swimmer, dived underwater again and surfaced several yards ahead of Babcock; this time he faced his enemy and again said, 'Hello, Tommy, sorry I'm not going to let you leave so soon.'

Babcock turned again and headed the other way, only to find Delany facing him again. This time, he swam to the left of Delany, who merely reached out and gently pushed Babcock's head underwater, releasing him almost immediately. Babcock spluttered and tried to stand but found that he was out of his depth. By now, he was frightened and trembling. He said in a shaky voice, 'Who are you, and what do you want?'

'Can't you guess? You tried to have me killed a few weeks ago?'

'Delany?'

'Correct.'

'Let me get out of here and we can talk.'

'We'll talk here. You sent your heavies to rape and kill my daughter Holly, they drowned her in the canal after they gang raped her and they killed her boyfriend. Now, it's your turn.'

'Babcock was by now desperate; he could feel his heart thumping against his chest, 'I didn't know what they were going to do, I just sent them to put the frighteners on, that's all. Are you going to kill me?'

As he said it, he made a lunge to the right of Delany in an attempt to get past. Delany again simply ducked Babcock's head under the water, but this time he held it for a few seconds before releasing him. Babcock came up choking and spluttering, he felt like his heart was on fire.

'OK, what do you want? Tell me what you want from me, anything, I'm worth a small fortune. Name your price.'

'I don't want your filthy money. You sent someone to clean Holly's flat afterwards, I want the name of that person.'

'You know we don't grass on each other, I can't tell you.'

Delany pushed his head under the water for a third time. As he came up, he gasped, 'OK, I'll tell you; it was an ex-cop called Gerald Nesbitt, he's been working for me for years.'

'Why did he work for you?'

'I did him a favour a few years ago and he owed me.'

'Who's he working for now?'

'I've passed him on to Frankie Maxwell.'

Delany had by now decided that he could not drown this pathetic old fool and swam away towards the steps and out of the pool. He could hear Babcock trying to catch his breath from the centre of the pool.

He retrieved his clothes from the lounge, switched the camera back on and began to leave the way he had entered, and as he reached the side of the gate house, he could hear Babcock still making loud choking noises. He looked towards the pool and saw him trying to climb the steps out, clutching his chest. He heard a loud cry of pain and Babcock slumped back into the water, where he lay face down. Delany watched for a few minutes and saw that Babcock was not moving.

Delany shrugged and said to himself, 'Ah, such is life,' and walked quietly away.

The pair still had a few days' holiday left, so they enjoyed the holiday resort, the food, the sunshine, and instead of the sangria, they used the local beer as a substitute.

Baldy met up with Crabby, as they had arranged previously. Crabby was clearly in a downcast and thoughtful mood.

'What's up, Ben?'

'Tommy's dead, he had a heart attack in the pool, it was the night when we last met. I got home that night and we'd had a few and I went straight to bed. I got up at seven to let the cleaner in. She came running back, she'd found him face down in the pool. Ann was flat out as usual, she takes sleeping pills, you know, I had to wake her and tell her the news. I must say, she took it well.'

'How do you know he had a heart attack?'

'The cops came and had a post-mortem done.'

Baldy probed deeper, 'You know, Tommy had a lot of enemies, are there no suspicious circumstances?'

'No, he was even seen on camera. He was on his own and collapsed in the pool, they say that he didn't drown, there was no water in his lungs. There was only one funny thing in my mind, although the cops made nothing of it. The camera has a timing device and it appeared to miss about half an hour's footage before he died, the cops just said it was a malfunction, at least I think that was the word they used. Anyway, they're not making anything of it; if they're happy, then so am I.'

'What next for you?'

'Dunno, Ann wants to stay here, so maybe I'll stay and look after her.'

Baldy reported the conversation back to Delany, who said, 'Great, job done, let's just enjoy the rest of our holiday, do your best to stay reasonably sober, Baldy.'

Chapter Twenty-Three

On his return, Delany travelled to Manchester to visit Paula in her office.

Because he had arranged to meet her in her office, she realised that this was going to be a business call. 'To what do I owe this pleasure, hang on, knowing you, will it be a pleasure?'

'I have some information for you. Do you know a Scenes of Crime Officer by the name of Gerald Nesbitt?'

'Yes, I've known Gerald for years, he was a detective on my staff until he retired. Why do you ask?'

'My information is that he also has another job on the side. He worked for Tommy Babcock, cleaning up after his yobs. Do you remember, I am sure you do, the effective way that Holly's flat was cleaned after the murders?'

'You're not saying the Gerard Nesbitt did that, are you?'

'That is exactly what I am saying.'

'Wait a minutes, I've just read that Tommy Babcock died of a heart attack in Spain and I know that you have just been away on holiday, where did you go?'

'Spain.'

'Did you have anything to do with the death of Babcock?'

'I spoke to Babcock briefly before he died, but, no, he died from a heart attack, a natural event. It was nothing that I could prevent, and it was from him that I got the information about Nesbitt.'

'Josh. I don't want to know anything more about that; in any case, Babcock is dead and, obviously, no longer able to bear witness, so you can't prove anything. All he has to do is deny it, and that's the end of the matter.'

'Normally, I would agree, but there's more, as the comedian once said. Nesbitt is now working occasionally for Frankie Maxwell.'

Paula was shocked. 'Maxwell is now the top dog controlling the drug trafficking in this area, we have been after him for months but have been unable to get anything on him. My god, we should have realised. There has been one local murder that we think he was linked to, where the house was cleaned in a similar way to Holly's flat.'

'You believe me now?'

'Still not certain about Nesbitt, but, yes, I believe you. This is now an operational matter, and I cannot officially involve you.'

'I'm happy to leave the matter entirely to you.'

Thinking aloud, Smithson said, 'I don't see the point of interviewing Nesbitt from what you have told me, the only way I can see to resolve this would be a phone tap, and for that, I need to apply to a judge.'

'I think you are spot on there. I have no other evidence than hearsay from a deceased person, we, or rather you, are going to have to start from the beginning.'

Smithson made an appointment to see the Chief Constable, she outlined what had been said to her by Delany, without revealing his identity, simply saying the source was believed to be reliable and had come from Babcock himself.

She was reluctantly given permission by the Chief Constable, saying, 'It is imperative to ascertain whether this is true or false. I admit that it is my fervent wish that it is false; however, if we have a rotten apple in our barrel, we need to root it out. Keep me informed.'

Smithson was a bit out of her depth with phone taps and the undercover sleuthing that went with it. Realising that she could not use the obvious expertise of Delany, she took Jerry Saunders, the expert in these matters, into her confidence.

They met in her office, and after telling him the full story, he said, 'Well, first of all, we can look at his recent telephone history. We don't need a judge's permission for that. There may be something there that will lead us to more, or less, suspicion than we already have, which I must say is very thin. I am hoping it is not true, I met him for a couple of pints recently, I'm now wondering if he was pumping me for information.'

They agreed to meet again when this had been arranged and the information gained had been assessed.

That weekend, Beverley visited Delany at his home. 'Dad, have you seen the Manchester evening paper?'

'No, why?'

'I have a copy here, I'll read an extract. "Divers have found a body in Nibs Quarry," it says. "The body has been identified by the police as Ramsay Simms, a known Manchester drug dealer who had just completed a term of imprisonment for drug-related offences. All indications are that he had driven into the flooded quarry, where he had drowned. No one else is being sought in relation to this incident."'

'Well,' Delany replied, 'he appears to have committed suicide, poor lamb. Perhaps we should go out for a meal this evening to commiserate his passing.'

Two weeks later, Saunders visited Smithson in her office.

'I'm sorry to say that I have some positive news for you, we have taken Nesbitt's phone records back as far as we can. If we go back to the rape and murder of Holly Delany and the murder of her boyfriend, Nesbitt had a call from an unidentified mobile phone in the very early hours of that morning. Obviously, we have no idea who that call was from or what it was about. However, that spurred us on. I don't know if you are aware or not, but just down the road in Sale, the flat of a man who the local police suspected was trying to break into the Manchester drug scene was broken into and the body of this man was found by his family the following morning, he had been garrotted in his bed. The thing is that his flat had been cleaned in a similar manner to that of Holly's.'

'Smithson interjected, 'How can we connect that to Nesbitt?'

'Well, we can't yet, but what I can tell you is that Nesbitt received a call from a mobile which we are unable to identify, again in the early hours of that same morning; meaning, that it is now becoming more likely that the allegations made against him are true. I think that it is now time for you to apply to a Judge-in-Chambers for a clandestine phone tap.'

Smithson applied for the appropriate authority, and it was granted.

She had a further meeting with Saunders.

'I'm going to need all the help I can get from you now Jerry.'

'Don't worry,' he replied, 'This is now a priority. I have spoken to the chief, and I am with you all the way, we need to tread carefully on this one, we can't turn out every time Nesbitt gets an unidentifiable phone call, or he will soon know that we are on to him. I suggest that we only react to any strange mobile call he receives most likely late at night or in the early hours, directing him to any address out of the blue and for no obvious reason, then we go, agreed?'

'Yes, this could be a long and difficult operation, we are going to have to detail an officer to listen to and assess all his calls night and day. We could, of course, bring him in and interview him.'

'No,' Saunders replied, 'that way, he denies it and we have lost any chance of nailing him. You and I are going to have to be on standby at any time to turn out to this. I will, of course, brief some of my most trusted staff to assist.'

Josh Delany and Paula Smithson met for dinner in a Manchester hotel, where she outlined the progress made and future plans regarding Nesbitt.

'Paula, whatever happens, I can't thank you enough.' As he looked at her, he realised that his feelings for her were growing stronger by the day, he had not thought that he would ever love another woman again after the death of his wife, but now he was certain that was not true.

The way she was looking at him suggested that maybe his feelings towards her were reciprocated, she said, 'Where are you staying tonight?'

He replied, 'Oh, I was just going to drive home, that's why I'm only having one glass of wine.'

'I can only have one glass as I may be turned out at any time, but please help me empty the bottle and stay with me tonight.'

He did, and she was not turned out, what a splendid night it became. In fact, it was so good that from that evening, he occasionally stayed with her in the small detached bungalow in Sale, and they became lovers.

It was two months later when the call came at one o'clock in the morning and on an occasion when Delany was absent. The caller was Jerry Saunders, and he gave her an address in Altrincham, saying, 'Paula, this looks like it, he'd had a call just giving the address, The Smithy, Eaves Lane, nothing else. I'm turning out but I've further to travel that you, my staff, are also turning out, but it may take a little time, I suggest that you delay your turnout by about twenty minutes to give us time to catch up with you.'

Paula was dressed, and within five minutes, she snatched up her police radio phone and set off towards the address given; it took only ten more minutes to get there, and on her arrival, she saw Nesbitt's car parked on the road outside what appeared to be a very expensive-gated detached house set back well off the road. The gates were open, and she could see a long drive leading to a large house.

She parked immediately behind Nesbitt's car, and as she was about to get out of her vehicle, a large white van pulled at speed from the drive and on to the road, the vehicle took off towards Manchester at a fast rate, tyres screaming as it did so.

Smithson was slightly shocked, but her policing instincts took over and she noted the vehicle's registration number and jotted it on the back of her hand.

She got on the radio and gave the operator her position and the make and number of the van, stating the urgency of the matter as she suspected that a serious crime had been committed, urging any officers to take care when stopping the van and approaching the occupants.

She went alone towards the house, she saw that lights were on, the front door was open and the house appeared to be very quiet.

As she entered the house through the unlocked front door, she realised that in her hurry, she was completely unarmed, she had even forgotten to bring her asp.

Noises could be heard from the upstairs, but downstairs, all seemed quiet. She crept up the wide staircase as silently as she could to the landing at the top. She could hear sounds coming from one of the bedrooms in front of her.

She could smell a very strong odour of bleach. Paula quietly opened the bedroom door and saw in front of her a large man wearing a white plastic overall, hood and gloves, with his back to her, spraying a substance on to the bed. There was no one else in the room.

'Mr Nesbitt, I presume.'

The man clearly shocked, turned quickly towards her; as he did so, she heard the door close noisily behind her. She turned and saw a tall dark-haired young man behind her. He moved forward and grabbed her by the arms; the large man in white also moved towards her with the spray gun in his hand, shouting, 'Open her mouth,' the younger man changed his hold and grabbed her around the waist with his left hand, at the same time taking her under the nose with his right hand to attempt to open her mouth.

Paula had not spent many hours in the gym training for nothing. She bit his right hand as hard as she could, at the same time twisting out of his grip, and as she did so, the large man sprayed his bleach gun, intending that it should fill her mouth and incapacitate her. Instead, the spray hit the younger man full in the face, and he screamed and fell to the floor, holding his eyes and face in obvious agony.

Nesbitt was still holding the bleach spray. Paula dodged quickly behind him, he was much slower than her; he turned, and as he did so, she kicked him between the legs. He dropped the spray, shouting in pain and holding himself. Paula picked up a metal bedroom lamp and struck Nesbitt hard on the head, he dropped to the floor unconscious, alongside his now weeping associate.

Jerry Saunders and two of his team burst into the bedroom, he took in the scene before him and said, 'Wow.'

Smithson rang for an ambulance, saying, 'We are going to have to get these two to the hospital before we can make any sense of this.'

At the Accident and Emergency Unit, Nesbitt was quickly assessed, he recovered consciousness but was very groggy, the doctor stated that he must be admitted to keep a check on his head injury overnight.

Saunders cautioned and arrested him, arranging an officer to guard him during his confinement, but the younger man was discharged, still in great discomfort, but the doctor was happy that there would be no long-term effects. He was whisked off by Saunders and his staff to the Central Detention Centre.

Smithson was about to leave the hospital herself and was walking through the exit doors when an ambulance drew up outside, escorted by two police cars.

A woman was stretchered into the hospital by ambulance men, and a young policewoman got out of one of the cars, holding the hands of two very young children. Smithson recognised her as Constable Wendy Taylor.

The officers said, 'Will you hang on, ma'am these two need to be checked out, they have a few bumps and bruises, nothing serious.'

Smithson re-entered the hospital, the policewoman came back to her after a few minutes and said, 'When we got the radio message from you, we all realised that it must be something very serious, so just about every police vehicle in Manchester was on the alert, the van was spotted on Chester Road and the driver refused to stop. It became a massive chase all through Manchester and Salford, then back into Manchester again; eventually, they were stopped using a stinger in Fallow field.'

Taylor stopped for breath, and Smithson said, 'Is that why these children and the woman have been brought here?'

'Yes, I'll get to that. Fortunately, we had an armed response team backing us up during the chase, when two men jumped from the van, they were armed with handguns. The armed response lads were on them in a flash, and they dropped their guns. In the back of the van, we found a third member of the gang and the woman and her children, she was obviously drugged, tied up and out of it, the kids had been thrown around in the van and were bruised but otherwise all right.'

As she said that, a nurse brought the two young girls, four and five years old, to Constable Taylor, saying they are discharged into her custody and that their mother will be staying with us for a while, 'She is still unconscious, but stable.'

Smithson said, 'Any sign of rape or other sexual abuse?'

'No, she has multiple bruises to her face and body. I understand she has been thrown about in the back of a van, but the facial bruises look more like a beating with fists.'

At the detention centre, she liaised with Saunders who had just finished interviewing the younger man.

'He is called Ivan Novak, he is not one of the gang members and, so far as we know, has no previous criminal history. He only came into the country very recently and is very frightened, he seems to be telling us everything he knows. He normally works for Serge Brednovic and his family as a gardener, cook and general factotum; Serge is a multi-millionaire who owns the house, he is away in Brussels on business. Novak, it seems, was befriended by Tim Carr, one of the lads we have in custody. He was unhappy with the wages he was getting and was talked into helping to kidnap Mrs Brednovic and her kids for ransom. He says that he was assured that no harm would come to them and that he would be well paid for his assistance.'

'Do you think that Carr is the main mover behind this?'

'No, he's up and coming in the drug world, but not, I am sure, the leader of this outfit.'

Smithson said, 'Scenes of Crime are at the house now, do we know when the owner is due back?'

'Yes, that's the point, he is due at Manchester Airport at ten this morning, and it seems that this gang had timed the kidnapping for the morning of his return. I'm going to be tied up here for a while with interviews, Novak is telling us all he knows, but the others are saying nothing as of yet. I wonder if you would mind meeting Mr Brednovic at the airport.'

Ten o'clock saw Paula Smithson waiting outside Terminal 3 at Manchester Airport, holding a card with the name Brednovic in large letters. At ten forty-five, a very smart middle-aged man with dark slightly greying hair walked towards her, looked slightly perturbed and said, 'My name is Brednovic, are you looking for me?'

Serge Brednovic?'

'Yes.'

Smithson introduced herself and said, 'I don't want you to worry too much, but there is no easy way of saying this, your wife is in hospital following an attempted kidnapping, she is stable and not causing any concern. Your children are safe and in our care, please come with me.'

Brednovic followed her to the airport police station where she put him fully in the picture explaining that his children were at the central police station being looked after by a very kind young police woman and she offered to take him to the hospital to see his wife, which he gratefully accepted.

He was greatly shocked but, at the same time, very relieved that his family were safe.

At the hospital, his wife, though battered and sore, was ready for discharge, and she was very happy to see her husband.

The house had been cleared by the Scenes of Crime Officers. The couple were reunited with their children and taken home by the local police.

Paula could at last go home and get some long-awaited sleep.

After five hours of blessed sleep, Paula Smithson returned to the hospital, where she found that Nesbitt had recovered consciousness and was about to be discharged into the custody of the police. Now that he was aware of his surroundings, Smithson again cautioned and reminded him that he was under arrest and what for. By now, he was aware of the serious trouble he was in. He was taken to the Central Detention Centre.

Over the next eight hours, he was interviewed by Smithson; at first, he was not forthcoming and under instruction from his solicitor and answered with the curt reply, 'No comment.'

However, as the day passed from morning into afternoon, both he and his solicitor realised the amount of evidence which was stacked up against him and the fact that he was in for a very long prison sentence, which would probably be extended by his lack of co-operation. It would also be made more traumatic by the fact that he had been a police officer.

At one o'clock that afternoon, on the recommencement of the interview and on the recommendation of his solicitor, he said, without any questions being asked, 'I want to turn Queen's evidence, but before I do, I want to be assured that when I go to prison, which I know will be inevitable, that the police will speak up for me, tell the judge that I have co-operated fully and that I should be given a shorter sentence and that I should be allocated a prison where I can go into protective custody.'

Smithson said, 'You must understand that I cannot guarantee anything, but I will ensure that the judge is made aware of your co-operation.'

That same evening, Paula and Josh met at their favourite restaurant, where she told him about the interview with Nesbitt, who she said had been singing like the fabled canary and had brought down the whole operation of Frankie Maxwell.

He and his senior gang members were now in custody. Maxwell had unwisely decided to go into the business of kidnapping. The plan was to take Brednovic for one million pounds, which, according to their co-opted very junior partner Novak, he could easily afford.

A week later, Delany was at his home when he was visited by Baldy, he was incredulous when Delany related to him all that had gone on in Manchester, then Baldy said, 'First of all, the wife has chucked me out permanently, she does not want me to darken her doorstep again,' he said smiling.

'You don't look unduly worried about that.'

'No, I'm not, and I have something else to tell you. I have heard from Crabby Johnson, who I must start to call Ben. Do you remember that he was worried that he would have to return to Manchester following the death of Babcock?'

'Yes, I remember, what's new?'

'Well, apparently, he has become, shall we say, emotionally involved with Ann Babcock and they are now living together permanently at the villa, he is happy as Larry and, apparently, so is she. When Tommy passed away,' he coughed into his hand, 'she gave a great display of emotion, tears at the funeral, and all secretly, she was delighted when his body was found in the pool that morning.'

Delany smiled and said, 'Wow, that's a turn up for the books.'

'I have not finished, my friend. Crabby, ahem, Ben has asked me to take over his duties at the gatehouse to the villa on a full-time basis, he just wants me as a neighbour and drinking partner, I have accepted.'

'Good for you.'

'Now, the next bit, you will of course remember his two sons.'

'Yes, what were their names, oh, yes, Tom and Jerry.'

'Now, now, Josh, well, they are completely reformed characters following their encounter with us, they are also living at the villa and working at bar jobs in the resort, I want your promise that you will leave them alone.'

'They have paid their dues, I have no further interest in them.'

'I don't want them ever to know of my part in their, shall I say, reform.'

'I have something to tell you, I am going to ask Paula Smithson to marry me, I don't know what her answer will be, but I hope for the best.'

'Good for you, Josh, the very best of luck.'

Epilogue

He met Paula that evening in their favourite restaurant, he was armed with a ring and hoped that his request would not be spurned. As it happened over a glass of brandy at the end of the meal and he was about to produce the ring from his pocket, Paula took him completely by surprise.

'I will have thirty years' service in two months' time and I was thinking of retiring from the police. I have always had a fancy to run a small hotel or boarding house in the Lake District.'

'I could quite happily go along with that.'

She smiled and said, 'If I sold my house and you sold yours, we would, I am certain, have enough money to buy a nice place where we could entertain our guests in the summer and live quietly in the winter.'

She saw the ring as he pulled it from his pocket, saying, 'Before you commit yourself to me, I think you should know what I have been up to these past few months.'

Paula put her finger to her lips and said, 'I only need to know one thing before I say yes. Is it over?'

'Yes.'